I0672785

Artificial Intelligence:

The Final Dominion

SE Flint & R Rajkumar

Copyright ©2018 by S.E. Flint and R. Rajkumar. All rights reserved. No part of this book may be reproduced, scanned, or distributed in any printed or electronic form without permission. Please do not participate in or encourage piracy of copyrighted materials in violation of the author's rights. Purchase only authorized editions.

Cover by Dissect Designs, dissectdesigns.com Copyright©2018

Copyediting by Joshua Gray

This is a work of fiction. Names, characters, most businesses, places, events, locales, and incidents are either the products of the author's imagination or used in a fictitious manner. Any resemblance to actual persons, living or dead, is purely anecdotal. Actual historical events regarding Artificial Intelligence, computer technology and internet development are true, including the names of movies.

Acknowledgements

We are grateful to Dr. Nisha Manek, for her unwavering inspiration and friendship; Steve Scott for his wealth of knowledge; for Derek Murphy's passion for writing and book publishing, inspiring DIY videos and dedicated interaction on his social media page; Dr. Githa Jayaram and Mr. Chandru, for their conversations and encouraging us even after listening to our primitive first draft chapters; a special thanks to the Ooty Library and Book Club—for such inspiration, friendship, and lively conversations. A deep gratitude for our teachers and professors--thank you for such wonderful encouragement and inspiration. A warm thank you to our families and friends, both human and zoological, for their support and love. A special thanks to Mom, for that extra help. Without the Divine presence in our lives, we would be without direction.

S. E. Flint and R. Rajkumar

And a special thanks to Gale Ann Hurd for the long conversations and for kindling my interest in AI, robotics, and futurology, without which this book idea might not have occurred.

R. Rajkumar

Dedicated to those who have
an interest in the benevolent
use of technology.

Acknowledgements

We are grateful to Dr. Nisha Manek, for her unwavering inspiration and friendship; Steve Scott for his wealth of knowledge; for Derek Murphy's passion for writing and book publishing, inspiring DIY videos and dedicated interaction on his social media page; Dr. Githa Jayaram and Mr. Chandru, for their conversations and encouraging us even after listening to our primitive first draft chapters; a special thanks to the Ooty Library and Book Club—for such inspiration, friendship, and lively conversations. A deep gratitude for our teachers and professors--thank you for such wonderful encouragement and inspiration. A warm thank you to our families and friends, both human and zoological, for their support and love. A special thanks to Mom, for that extra help. Without the Divine presence in our lives, we would be without direction.

S. E. Flint and R. Rajkumar

And a special thanks to Gale Ann Hurd for the long conversations and for kindling my interest in AI, robotics, and futurology, without which this book idea might not have occurred.

R. Rajkumar

Dedicated to those who have
an interest in the benevolent
use of technology.

1

February 1989, a mere 4 months before they were due to defend their thesis papers, five friends traveled to a cybernetics conference at The Institute in Boston. They had pooled their money for this occasion. Andrei Sokolov, a friend and colleague of their mentor, was making a somewhat rare appearance from the then, U.S.S.R.

An enthusiastic Marcus Coates and Hugh Bingham stood up to welcome Andrei as he entered the hotel restaurant. Andrei Sokolov was a master code writer and brilliant computer engineer. Marcus and Hugh had the pleasure of listening to his and Jill Truhn's speeches during the same conference two years earlier.

"Professor Sokolov, please join us," offered Marcus as he eagerly reached out to shake hands. The usually subdued Marcus offered a broad smile.

"Yes, of course, I'd like that very much, but only for a short while. My wife is here with our child. They'll be down in a moment." The friends looked at Andrei with surprise.

"Congratulations are in order!" Marcus nearly shouted. Sheila Wei and Sapna Chatterjee smiled demurely and spoke in unison, "Congratulations, Sir!"

"Thank you." Andrei smiled shyly as he sat with the youth. Three years before his marriage to Jill, Andrei would have never imagined the happy turn that his life had taken. He reflected for a moment while the conversation lulled.

"We've developed something that we thought might be of interest to you, Professor Sokolov," began Jay Mori.

"It's an alternative protocol to the internet," blurted out Hugh Bingham.

"Tell me more," he said eagerly.

Upstairs in their room, leaning over the bed, Jill Truhn changed her baby's diapers quickly. She distracted her boy with funny sounds. The baby gurgled and giggled at his mother's faces.

"My little Champion!" Jill cooed as she leaned over to blow raspberry kisses on his belly. Behind her, she heard a door click. The boy giggled with Jill.

"Honey, did you forget something?"

As Jill turned to look, three masked assailants, two men and a woman rushed at her. Jill picked up the diaper bag and threw it, contents spilling out over the carpet. The baby startled and screamed.

"Someone shut that baby up!" said the tall man. They grabbed at Jill.

"NO!" she shouted.

Jill stepped on the tall man's foot and kneed him in the groin and scratched his face. His mask fell off as he cried out, "Bitch!"

The other two grabbed a hold of Jill's flailing arms. She haplessly kicked at them. The masked red-headed woman rushed at Jill with a needle, "Steady." The syringe filled with fast-acting curare dispersed into Jill's system. The taller man held her sprawling body off the ground for thirty seconds until she became silent, limp. Jill was conscious but couldn't act.

"No! Ja…" Jill's words couldn't come out. She lost strength. I know him! How is this happening? My baby! God protect my baby! Andrei…

The attackers dressed as hotel cleaning staff stuffed the petite brunette into the laundry cart. Jill's piercing blue eyes looked up at the tall assailant's face.

"Cover her face," he said.

"I thought you could handle this," sneered the other man.

"Shut up."

They left the crying baby in the stroller, with the door ajar. Baby Nikko's cries echoed down the hallway as they rolled his mother away and exited through the hotel service elevator.

Downstairs, Andrei Sokolov read and signed the non-disclosure agreement. He carefully folded his copy around the floppy disk and pocketed it in his wool blazer.

"Thank you, what an honor. I look forward to addressing this program." He paused and looked at his watch. "Looks like Jill is occupied. Our baby is still very young"

"Excuse me. Dr. Sokolov," the maître d's urgent hushed tone stopped the conversation, "there's an urgent matter. Please come." Andrei left immediately. They half-ran to the elevator.

"Room 531?"

"Yes," answered a nervous Andrei.

"Housekeeping heard your baby crying and went to investigate," he said in a hushed tone as they entered the elevator. Andrei's facial muscles tightened. He could hear his baby crying as soon as the elevator stopped on the 5th floor. The long hallway seemed endless.

"She left me only 15 minutes before to change the boy's diapers."

"Yes, I saw. I've called the authorities." The maître d' paused, "You'll find her."

Andrei remained silent as the maître d' pushed the door open.

"Don't touch anything. Just take your boy out of his stroller."

Andrei rushed in and froze, surveying the room. Nikko's red tearstained face anticipated his father's comfort.

"There. There. There. Papa is here, my dear Nikko. Papa is here." Andrei took his boy out of the stroller and cradled him. The boy rubbed his face on his father's neck. Andrei Sokolov's eyes glazed over, clutching the little baby.

Jill Truhn's parents arrived from Washington D.C. the next day. The Truhns carried grave expressions. Andrei couldn't hide his own feelings of anxious fear, uncertainty about the future. Their relationship had warmed up after the birth of their grandson Nikko. Andrei, after all, was an older man without definite goals, a foreigner from behind the Iron Curtain.

"My daughter goes missing. There were signs of a struggle. You filed a missing person's report. You gave comfort to your toddler, who was also a witness; you fulfilled your professional responsibilities, dealt with the press and you called us. Well done, son. I couldn't imagine accomplishing that much under such pressure," said Jack Truhn.

He continued, "How do you plan to stay in the U.S. when your visa clearly isn't long enough?" asked Marie Truhn.

Dumbfounded, Andrei stammered, "I...I haven't thought about it yet. I was hoping I could stay in D.C. until they found Jill..." his voice trailed off.

"We know what a strain this must be for you. Why don't we take little Nikko for a while? We have more experience looking after a baby." said Marie in a tight, shrill voice.

Something in her tone of voice didn't give Andrei a good feeling. I'll never part with my boy! he thought.

"Let me think this over. Didn't sleep last night. We'll see you tomorrow. I hope they have encouraging news about Jill."

"Tomorrow will be a better day," said Jack while exchanging glances with his wife as he embraced Andrei. Marie slowly stooped down to catch a view of her sleeping grandson.

"Yes, of course. See you tomorrow. Good night," said Andrei with a tired voice.

Andrei rolled the sleeping baby in the stroller towards his new room. As Andrei disappeared around the corner, Jack held on to Maria's hand as she unsteadily sat down again at the table.

"Do you believe him?" asked Jack.

"Of course! How could you say such a thing?" Maria snapped.

2

Professor A looked in the mirror while adjusting his tie. Too formal for the first day of class? Blue instead of red? he wondered.

"Darling, the Air Drone is here," his wife's gentle voice asserted, "and you look great, as always. The red tie, most definitely."

"Mmmm. I love you, too." Professor A gazed over at his wife of almost sixty years. She was wise and strong; she had given him three healthy children and almost single-handedly raised them, given his work schedule in earlier days.

As he stood in front of his class, Professor A's heart swelled with pleasure. The zip link pinged a gentle tone to alert the professor that the microphone and lens were live, broadcasting his class to other regions in the Planetary Union, university affiliates on earth, mining outposts, and moon settlements. He opened class with the Union's pledge. All students stood up and opened their palms and spoke with a solemn voice:

"As a loyal Planetary Union member, I pledge my heart for the common good: peace, justice, truth, and right action; equality in humanity; integrity with natural resources. May this prevail forever and forever."

Earth history had come a long way since Professor A's childhood, when countries gloated over their budding space programs, the ones riddled with troubles. Safe space travel was as much a reality as was instant communication—beyond the speed of light. Professor A watched Star Wars in a movie theatre with sticky floors, in the humid Illinois summer of 1977. He never thought that he'd live to use the actual technology. Many gadgets came up from nowhere and disappeared in a blink. Tablet computers of the early part of the century were a good example.

His Earth Civilization course was popular; earth had almost reached the cusp of doom by 2022, and its brilliant future wasn't certain. How long would it take to raise yet another civilization if this one had fallen, another thousand years? We were lucky this time. How many times has this happened on earth before? he wondered. His thoughts were interrupted by a loud laugh. Oh, one of those kinds of students in the class this time.

"The Planetary Onion," a red-headed youth named Jordan said out loud in one of those voices that can't whisper. A few snickers could be heard in the classroom. Their sounds reverberated throughout the universe via the zip link communications. Shocked students watched and waited. This kind of outburst was not tolerable. Professor A ignored him and began:

"History is the record of the time that went past us in different directions. The winners and the oppressed told it from different points of view, from the different parts of the world. Dear students, in this era of time, what they called 'civil' was a gross overstatement. This exaggeration bordered on hyperbole. Still, in these times, the mind-set was a might is right premise, vestiges of the Paleolithic era. Yes, as a modern society, they had overcome the difficulties of being cavemen and women in practice and convenience. Huge human migrations led to cultural diversity, a blending of ideologies. Technological advances made the world small. Advances over the span of centuries, across the world led the populous to modern society. But during this time in many parts of the world, the husband still had specific privileges over the wife. It was legal to raise a hand or fist to her," Professor A paused for a dramatic effect, "and even by 2017, a few South American countries lobbied for mass sterilization of the feminine gender." The class gasped.

He stepped up with one robust motion onto his chair and then to his sturdy desk. The cameras followed him. Professor A beat his chest to drive the point home. The shocked students looked on. From his lofty vantage point, Professor A continued.

"The postmodern era, or Pre-Link, as historians like to call it, was a time of desperation. Neglect in waste management, in such ways, that garbage avalanches killed people and inundated whole villages. Debris in space reached a tipping point. Kessler's theory was proven right—that more than 20,000 artificial objects better known as space trash in both the geosynchronous and low earth orbits impeded the path of some 2000 operational satellites, and in some cases causing collisions. Disinformation in the media caused confusion about simple truths. Political concerns caused general petty backbiting among political parties and nations. Feudal ruling systems sat in the cradle with nuclear arsenals. This was a time when earth ran scorching temperatures. Storm velocities grew. Firestorms consumed whole towns and villages. The cave man still lived inside the modern human psyche. A whirlpool of disharmony ended with disaster."

Professor A stepped down and with arms crossed, leaned on the corner of his desk. Students sat upright in their chairs, eyes on his. He pursed his lips and examined their faces one by one, wondering if this was too much information.

"Yes, my dear students, there was a problem with mindset." Professor A looked in the general direction of Jordan and his friends.

"Some of you mock the Planetary Union? Your grandparents, then dubbed the Millennials, were the only age group in world history as we know it to grow up with advanced technology and know how to use it. They were the better-informed citizen. This Planetary Union was built on the backs of their ideals. They weren't afraid to make the change from an antiquated Industrial Age to an enlightened Information Age." The class was still, and the zip link transmission was clear.

"But, dear students, I'm getting ahead of myself. One decade before the Millennials were born, there was a woman who aspired and dared to challenge an old, crumbling system. Her name was Jill Truhn."

3

A massive cloud spanned across the sky as far as he could see. Hugh Bingham increased his driving speed into the storm, arriving at his target location after dark. The wind had shifted into a strong downdraft, pelting icy rain. Hugh jumped out of the vehicle. His thick parka protected his body; he ignored the sting to his face. Tree branches danced in a harried frenzy as he heaved the 80-pound pack onto his back and turned, abandoning his car and his life as he knew it. Bolts of lightning fell around him, making contact with a nearby tree. Shattering wood crackled with bright illumination, lighting up the sky. He covered his face. Up ahead, Hugh saw a human figure. His headlamp didn't reach the 20 yards. The unrecognizable path led him across slippery stones. He stumbled and went down on one knee to regain his leverage. Hugh Bingham was certain that nobody followed him.

"Over here, Dude!" someone shouted.

"Hugh, this way!" Hugh didn't recognize the voice that came from the stormy darkness.

"Hugh! Over here." Lightning crashed down beyond the river. Sparks from the transformer shot out in every direction. Hugh jolted with the movement. His eyes flickered, opening to the new dawn.

"Sheeze," he murmured, wiping sweat from his brow, and rolling over to turn off his alarm clock.

The ruthless Chicago winter chill bore down as students waited outside. The University of Illinois solicited a new group of masterminds, North America's most advanced postgraduate program in computer sciences. U.S. intelligence, the Agency, had a strong presence seeking recruits from this program.

There stood light blonde Hugh Bingham with other hopefuls, squinting into the icy wind. A security guard rushed over to open the doors. Cold hands and noses followed the leader who carried a large manila folder. The graduate student-elects were silent.

"Sorry about that. Please form a semicircle around me. Can you hear me?" she called with a slight crackle in her voice. The tired and dazed eyes fixed upon her with a glassy anticipation. Marcus Coates ran up to the door. He looked lanky and awkward in his dark parka and caused a mild commotion as he slid into his place in the back of the group, next to a petite Asian woman.

"Are you settled in back there yet? Listen up! Welcome to University of Illinois, Chicago. Our motto here is 'Teach, research, serve, care...' her voice faded out. Marcus looked over at the young woman standing next to him. She had brown skin and long flowing wavy brown hair. Her long eyelashes framed soft dark brown eyes.

"Pay attention!" she said, winking both eyes at Marcus as she looked up at him and smiled.

"Right." Marcus fumbled, "Sorry."

"No offense taken," she said with a sultry voice.

The students met their mentors and other personnel. These future scientists would learn new technical skills, details that would catapult them into the 21st Century. Marcus Coates excelled and graduated Summa Cum Laude from The Institute in Boston. The beautiful dark-haired woman gazed across the room at Marcus and then averted her eyes to the floor when he reciprocated her gaze.

"Hi. I'm Hugh," said a young man, interrupting Marcus' moment. Marcus shook Hugh's extended hand.

"Hi. Marcus."

"Hope I wasn't interrupting anything," Hugh said with a smile, "or anything yet."

"The girl, sure. I'm looking forward to this program. Just think, how technology will change in the next 30 years?"

"I like you. You're a forward thinker," said Hugh.

"Something tells me you are too." Marcus smiled.

4

Two summers before her disappearance, Jill Truhn had spent Spring and Summer contemplating. Even though she carefully directed her life in a purposeful manner, the experiences she had called meaningless, weren't. This conflicted position gave her more reflection about her most recent actions: namely, losing control at the Cyber conference. Jill dialed her mom on the telephone.

"Mom, I'm prego."

"You're what?" replied Marie Truhn, "Are you learning Italian?"

Jill laughed, "I wish..." and hesitated and continued. "Mom, I have something important to tell you."

"Please, darling. Whatever it is, I'm with you," reassured her mother.

"I'm pregnant."

The silence on the phone line lasted for a good 20 seconds. Marie took a sip of her hot coffee. Jill squirmed and dared not say another word to her mother until she processed the information.

"We are all children of God. We are not perfect. And oftentimes we can't control ourselves. Darling? Are you there?"

"Yes, Mother, I'm listening."

"So, we're going to be Grandparents! You've been blessed, and so has our family."

Jill started to cry with relief. This was one instance that she wouldn't adapt herself to societal norms; being a single mother would be difficult in many ways.

"I love you, Mom."

"I love you, too, darling. I'll find a way to pass this good news on to Dad. You know how protective he is..." her voice faltered.

No, she hadn't gotten pregnant to entrap a man. She had taken all the necessary precautions but couldn't quite understand how it was that she still was able to conceive. She knew that age 30, accidental pregnancy was a lame excuse. Still, she couldn't understand how it happened, because she had used two kinds of protection. Deep inside of her, something grew.

Andrei Sokolov. Jill couldn't stop thinking about him. No matter how much she put him out of her mind, he drifted back in. She felt the magnetic pull. Her heart felt so full when she thought of him. Funny how this works, she mused, for the first time I know what love is, he's gone. They had exchanged numbers, but he didn't call. Jill couldn't bring herself to pick up the telephone. If he's interested in me, he will call. Please call, Andrei. She wanted to share the spark of life that was multiplying and dividing inside of her. Jill wanted nothing more than a stable life, a life that was in order.

I want my child to have both parents present. She closed her eyes. Jill drifted into a deep sleep.

Meanwhile, across the Atlantic Ocean, the Moscow ice was beginning to thaw. Andrei looked out his window. He took in the sunshine while sipping from a piping hot cup of tea. His thoughts drifted towards the United States. He still was in disbelief that he had been allowed to go. He had met wonderful people and made a few strong business contacts. Jill Truhn. Jill Truhn. Tru-hn, he thought. He gazed through the window into nothingness. Five minutes had lapsed. Andrei blushed—it was Jill Truhn who had made the trip so... Andrei had difficulty making sense of his experience.

Andrei had never had a girlfriend before. Jill was his first love. Where did this courage come from? he wondered. He imagined her face as she spoke at the conference. She was a good leader and communicator. Jill Truhn could recite code the way Russian poetess Vera Aglya wrote love poems. Steeping himself in sentimentality was not Andrei Sokolov's usual trait.

He recited the last stanza in Vera Aglya's poem "Love-Only" as like an LP stuck on repeat: "We pay only with our blood, but surely love only the soul - is true, and we love one love ... as the death of one love." Melancholy overtook Andrei's happy morning sunshine.

"Is this all there is?" he said out loud. He looked at the thriving green plant on his windowsill above the radiator heater. The clothing line stretched across his kitchen, drying his most recent wash. His food supply was fine, but it was increasingly difficult to get special items, like pork. In the big city, Moscow had most things available, but at a price. Andrei didn't support the black market for the hard to get items. His family owned property outside of the city. Often, he went to the dacha, his family's home to clear his head and fish in a nearby river. There, he pickled and canned his own fish.

Summertime in Russia was glorious. He imagined Jill next to him. On the riverbank of the Moskva somewhere near the Smolensk and Moscow Oblast borders, he'd lie with his love. They would play code word games next to the river that winds across Tolstoy's northwestern countryside like a ribbon in the wind.

Droplets of water glistened on his skin as he daydreamed. Andrei lazily rolled over and looked up. The deep blue sky spanned to infinity. He could feel his body sinking deeper into the blanket. For the first time in his adult life, Andrei Sokolov felt calm. The self-imposed fear of the unknown and pressure to perform melted.

Something inside him now was renewed. His new confidence, despite the changing world around him, gave him the idea to start up a company. He knew that his time at the university was on a clock, despite his position as a tenured academician. Job security in Russia was becoming shaky. In his mind, lovestruck

Andrei Sokolov mapped out a new future with Jill Truhn.

5

Professor A had a wistful look on his face. "Class, today I will give you a view into the inner workings of the creators of LINK language. LINK was the interface protocol built by five students at the University of Illinois. The year was 1989. Marcus Coates conceptualized a protocol with security at its heart for transmitting high-security communications over the internet."

"Their goal was to provide a networking protocol other than a TCP/IP, the up and coming internet protocol. Hugh Bingham, Sapna Chatterjee, Sheila Wei, and Jay Mori brilliantly contributed to Marcus' vision."

Jay Mori had taken a hardware class while he was home for the summer in California. Now he was intent on piecing together five computers so that they could experiment. The night was late. Sapna and Sheila's tiny rental apartment looked disheveled with computer parts, wires, and other hardware strewn across the floor. Two of the friends sat on the couch; milk crates held the monitors. Jay untangled the cables and set up the network.

The five experimented with different brands of computers—exploring support across the different platforms. Two computers ran DOS, a DOS 386 and a FlexOS 386. They bought a couple of computers that were beginning to gain popularity. The Peaxh, vying to dominate the market from a recent startup company. The Commander 64 was an obscure brand from America South West.

"Okay, I think this works," said Jay.

Sheila, who sat next to Sapna, bounced up and down with excitement.

"Ok guys. It looks like the program is easy for an average person to take home, plug in, and begin computing. 'Plug and play,' maybe they'll call it? I like that," quipped Sheila, who was good at marketing. "Ok, guys. Let's see what cross-platform integration will do. Are you all ready?"

Everyone nodded. Sapna had the oddball computer they nicknamed The Cyclops. Often it took off on its own tangent despite the commands. Sapna was the most patient one of the group and volunteered for the computer. She spoke to it as if it were a child. The others snickered.

"You will notice that if you speak nicely to the machine, it will perform better," she said in her defense.

"And I am sure that one day, scientific research will prove mental thoughts affect the results of mechanized simulators. I'd love to do research in that direction, but it's not my calling." Marcus rolled his eyes. The concept sounded too woo-woo for him.

"Ok kids let's do it!" said Jay.

Marcus was enthusiastic. "We need to have more options in this world…" His voice trailed off. Nobody

24

was listening, except for Sapna, who winked at him with both eyes. She knew what he meant.

"We're all connected. Networks are configured. Does everyone have the floppy disk with the program?" said Jay.

"Floppy disk...who gave it that name, anyway? I can't wait until we're using something smaller and less awkward. Floppies get damaged easily, like with heat." Marcus continued. Only Sapna listened and smiled.

Marcus and Sapna spoke their own language, and the other three knew that eventually, they'd end up together as life partners. The five friends understood that friendships should develop naturally, without imposing a social pressure.

"Ok, dear friends, let's load up LINK. Yes! That sweet anticipation," said Sapna, oblivious to romantic nuances. Marcus grinned; Jay caught on to Marcus' humor.

"Yeah, that's pretty...innocent..." Jay said under his breath. "Ok people. Fire it up!" said Jay, with emphasis on the dramatic.

The computers made processing sounds. The Cyclops loaded the LINK language program effortlessly.

"Finished?" asked Jay. Everyone nodded.

"Ok. Let's reboot, and rock-n-roll, kids!"

The friends looked at each other with eagerness.

"Cross your fingers," blurted out Marcus.

Sapna's eyebrows raised a little. Marcus, whose primary personal concern had been chronic feelings of hopelessness, now appeared to be feeling hopeful about something that mattered to him. She appreciated his efforts; he confided and trusted in her. She knew how much effort he put into making good changes and turning his life around. Their eyes met. Sapna smiled back at him.

All computers rebooted successfully. The computers linked across all the different platforms. The Cyclops even ran well. The Peaxh and the Commander 64 offered flawless reports when checked.

The five then tested for networking capabilities. Marcus couldn't stop smiling. He considered this program a viable product on the open market. Jay didn't think that the time was yet right to release it—if at all. The friends hadn't yet come to a consensus decision and were bound by a non-disclosure and proprietary agreement among themselves.

"The essence of this unification would eventually make all forms of computers or anything with an electronic operating system, compatible. LINK brought to light a common language within all complex networks and after 2010, Android and other similar software included. This different protocol helped other networks to operate in the same physical network space."

Professor A stopped speaking in frustration. His students didn't seem to notice. Their eyes glazed over with his information dump--overloaded. What is it with this generation? Was it the effect of technology from a young age with constant EMF exposure? he wondered.

6

Nobody was surprised that the Agency recruited Marcus Coates. He applied for an analyst position in computer systems and operations. The interview process was rigorous, he knew. Marcus' mind raced on. How much do they know about me?

Marcus had reason to be nervous. He had to come clean with the petty offenses. Of course, they probably know about it already, he reflected on his history. He wondered how he would be able to maintain his friendships, were he selected and hired. He would miss this closeness.

He stood straight, feeling somewhat awkward in his new clothes. His stare in the mirror told him more about himself in that moment. A wizened face, the sharp confident gaze looked back at him. No doubt. No doubt. No doubt, his regular mantra was on auto-play.

Marcus stepped into the foyer to meet with his friends before the interview. In this moment, Sapna Chatterjee knew something deep in her heart. She didn't say anything. Sapna was so proud of Marcus for what he had overcome in his personal life to get to this moment. This was nothing short of a miracle. She stood on her toes to pull the brown corduroy jacket square onto his broad shoulders, straighten his tie and fix his collar. She picked lint off of his pants. The other three looked on, pleased.

Marcus smiled and took Sapna's face into his big hands. He stroked a fallen piece of hair away from her full lips, looked into her eyes and asked, "May I?"

Sapna nodded. He kissed her on the lips. Her eyes closed as she relaxed into it, hands falling on his shoulders, knees going limp. Marcus held her closer into a tighter embrace. They kissed deeper and felt their hearts connect in an indescribable way. Their breath and pulse became one.

"I've always loved you," he whispered.

"Yeah. Me too you," she said softly. They studied each other's eyes

Suddenly, Marcus became self-conscious. He turned his head, "What?" he said to the others, who were trying to mind their own business. Jay and Hugh stepped forward and shook Marcus' hand.

"Congrats, and good luck, man!" said Jay.

Sheila grasped Sapna's hand, squeezed it and smiled at Marcus.

"Everything will turn out well! Go get 'em, Marcus!" she said.

"Thanks. 'I'll be back!'" he said in an affected tone, reminiscent of the Cyborg from the popular movie. His friends laughed.

"I'll see you later?" he said to Sapna with a new gentleness. Sapna nodded with a coquette smile. "Most definitely."

7

Meanwhile, in the arid Las Vegas desert, promising international robotics researchers congregated. They came from far to contend for a place in the world's Who's Who status in robotics. Researchers from the medical, industrial, and aerospace sectors co-mingled with manufacturers and representatives. The public came to witness the spectacle, as company reps plied their machines and brokered deals. Government agents mingled as customers. Robotic engineers schmoozed with lobbyists. The venue provided fertile grounds for plenty of distractions in a garish hotel. This was the 80s: anything went.

"We want to hire you as spies. You see, we want to know what our competitors are doing," angled Jason Zimmons to two unsuspecting sixteen-year-olds. Aside from business, the Las Vegas scene catered to Jason's obscure sensibilities. Las Vegas wasn't called Sin City for nothing; it spawned getting naughty as a tourist attraction.

A moment of nobility overcame Jason's newly divorced colleague, "Excuse us," he said to the girls as he pulled Jason away.

"Come on Jason. Can you say jailbait? Where are their parents, anyway? I'm going over to play roulette. Why don't you join me?"

"Age of consent is 16 here. I just spent 20 minutes hard selling them. You're blowing my plan. We can do anything we want here; we're in Vegas!" Zimmons glowered.

When not living in Las Vegas, Jason Zimmons stayed in Washington D.C. His finger pressed down on the pulse of politics. As a part time lobbyist who pandered to the politicians on Capitol Hill, Jason connected the underworld with unsuspecting government officials. He cut deals, brokered offers; bribes spawned new legislation and paid the price of advancement in technology. Of course, everything looked legitimate.

8

Nearing the last part of the third year, Sapna's parents had come to Chicago to visit her. For five days, the five friends met with Sapna's family in one capacity or another.

One night, crowded in the tiny kitchen, the friends watched Pushpa Chatterjee show how to eat Bengali food.

"You hold it like this..." Sheila, Hugh, Jay, and Marcus laughed at their clumsy attempts.

"You'll get it," Pushpa reassured them.

Sheila felt at home with Sapna's family and especially loved her mother—filling a gap in Sheila's heart from her own mother's premature departure from earth.

This was no ordinary time. The sharing of family and friendship strengthened and lifted the five friends' spirits. They sat on Sheila and Sapna's living room floor and ate together. Sapna's parents played old Bengali movie songs. The five watched Sapna's parents make eyes, scold, and coddle each other. It's true that their arranged marriage had developed into a deep love affair. Sapna one day hoped to have the same when she married. Her gaze momentarily landed on Marcus Coates, but quickly departed, for fear that her father would suspect something unusual between them.

"You know, Sapna, your father and I have a surprise for you," Pushpa said mysteriously after the last dish had been washed and dried. The door had just closed after the last boy. Sheila and Sapna rested on the couch.

"Oh Mama, what are you talking about?" Sapna did have an idea but didn't want to spoil her mother's excitement. Her father came out of her bedroom with a thick briefcase.

"Your mother and I," Gopal paused. "We think it is high time you consider marriage."

The smile on Gopal Chatterjee's face was sheepish, for he knew that she was an American citizen. But he believed that Sapna had retained a lot of the Indian culture from having spent her summers in India. Sapna and Sheila exchanged worried looks.

"I bid my goodnight to you all! I'm sure that you will find the right one, Sapna," Sheila squeezed Sapna's hand and gave her a solemn look. With a tiny bow, she was gone.

"I don't think that I'm ready for an arranged marriage, Papa." The silence in the modest living room hung heavily on Sapna's words,

From the moment of her girl-child's birth, the subject of education and marriage was every Indian mother's greatest preoccupation. Every mother's dream was that their daughter be safely protected and then entrusted to the groom and his family on the wedding day. The pressure doesn't stop until that day. An Indian mother who has an American-born-Indian daughter has many more variables: a culture that doesn't support strict religious values and practices, drugs, alcohol, rebellion, too many opportunities that could lead to sexual experimentation and other complexities that involve the female gender. Truly, Sapna bridged the two cultures perfectly.

"Papa, I have been meaning to talk to you about this. It's not easy to find a way to say this…I'm in love."

"What? How can this be? Who is it, that tall Marcus boy?" Gopal fumed, looking at his wife accusingly.

"Pushpa, it's all your fault! You indulged her. And you knew about it, didn't you?"

"Please keep your voice down Gopal. Not true. I knew nothing."

"Momma knew nothing. We've been good friends for two years. I've had a deeper feeling about him only recently."

"Nothing-doing! You're coming back with us to India. We'll marry you off and be done with it." Gopal's deep red face distorted with sweat. He sat down abruptly with his hand on his heart, gritting his teeth. He had been afraid of this but had trusted his daughter's sound ethics and behavior.

"The way he looks at you and speaks to you with such kindness and respect," Pushpa paused, "reminds me of someone else I know." Puspa looked over nervously at her beloved husband.

"Please tell us more about your friend Marcus." Pushpa's tone was gentle, wanting to understand her daughter. Sapna began to quietly cry. Gopal squirmed in his chair, noisily clearing his throat. His mouth was dry.

"You know, Marcus is a boy that we'd approve of." Sapna's mother pulled Sapna close and patted her over and over on her shoulder, repeating, "Little Sapna, Little Sapna, Little Sapna," in Bengali.

"Not this way. I have people to answer to. What will I tell them, that my daughter fell in love? That she has a love marriage?"

"Oh Gopal, stop with the dramatics. Sapna's an American citizen. This is an American tradition."

"I knew that I should have kept you in India while you were pregnant."

Pushpa started with his words. Under stress Gopal reverted to his parent's ideals, despite his modern beliefs and practices when he and Pushpa studied and worked the U.S.

"Don't go that direction. You know how much freedom you wanted when we came to the U.S. Now you're just like your parents: conservative, controlling, and ..." Pushpa stopped, paused, and redirected before she launched further injury.

"Cup of tea?" Pushpa got up and busied herself in the kitchen. Gopal and Sapna sat in silence. Pushpa returned with a tray of the hot milky substance and a few cookies.

"Sapna, you are a very sought-after girl," said Gopal with a softer, more persuasive tone while slurping his tea. For weeks, after each thick proposal envelope arrived, he practiced this performance. Somehow it wasn't working the way he had imagined. How could she be in love? He silently implored.

"Papa, please!" Sapna wouldn't budge from her position.

Gopal pulled out a file and began reading. "Rajiv Mohan Rajindranath. Clean practices. Computer science. The Institute. Studying his Ph.D."

"I don't want to know, Papa please," begged Sapna.

Gopal Chatterjee handed Sapna the photo. The tiny alarm clock on the table measured off time. Minutes passed while she studied his photo. She felt something deep inside, perhaps a guilt feeling. Duty to culture. Duty to parents. She sat for twenty minutes looking at the photograph.

"Mm. Strong jaw. Deep brown eyes. Slight smile. I like him," said Sapna with a decided finality.

"What? That's it? What about Marcus?" Pushpa Chatterjee urged.

"It will only confuse me. This is the man I'll call my husband. I almost feel disloyal if I look at another man after looking at Rajiv Mohan Rajindranath." Sapna's resigned monotonic voice ebbed. Her eyes glazed over, and she yawned.

"There are other young men who are more qualified. What about Marcus? You needn't make such a hasty decision, Sapna. You haven't prayed about it," urged Pushpa. Sapna's face covered with a dark shadow.

"This is your fault, Gopal," Pushpa's words cut and her gaze pierced.

"I will contact the astrologer for the best engagement date," Gopal said in a hushed tone. wiping his face with his hand.

"No, Gopal..."

Gopal looked at Pushpa, raised his finger with a dismissive hushing gesture, "Chshhht! I have spoken."

Nothing more was said about this subject.

9

The reception on the zip link proved a marked clarity on this day. The local students' bright smiles basked in the interplanetary connection. Professor A stood up from his chair.

"Well, when Andrei Sokolov conceived of the first version of AI in the mid-1990s, it was supposed to be a simple internet search engine utility with added features. He ported the AI version to the LINK protocol that the five students had written. The interface was good. Its job was to find and collate information and to bring out simple solutions for queries. In short, the AI gave intelligent answers instead of simple ones. It self-updated using available software from the internet, and of course collected data whenever possible. From that point, the software application grew through many rewrites and with time, included voice recognition for ease of use."

Andrei sat at his keyboard gazing at his computer screen.

"Excuse me, Dr. Sokolov?" interrupted his secretary. She was holding an envelope that had postage from the U.S. Andrei didn't hear her or perceive his secretary's presence. His eyes were focused on a fixed highlighted code that bore significance to his whole program.

"This is her heart," he mumbled.

"Dr. Sokolov?" his secretary repeated.

"Just leave it on the desk, please," muttered the focused computer scientist without looking up. Around him were 15 other computer engineers at desks across an expansive room, mostly men.

Andrei had created a life that gave him the freedom, and despite the dictum of the Russian economy, he did exceedingly well. He lived a highly disciplined life, raising a boy on his own, arranging a work schedule that revolved around Nikko's study schedule. He maintained his mental health with morning runs in the pastoral Russian countryside and yoga. Andrei's aging parents helped with what they could.

The U.S. court declared Jill Truhn dead and issued a death certificate three years after her disappearance. Andrei's nightmares varied. The scene changed, but it usually ended with the death certificate's dictum: Death in Absentia. He'd wake up sweaty and gasping for breath. Over the years, the words forced disappearance played inside Andrei's mind over and over.

Andrei didn't talk about America, and much less have the desire to ever return. His memories kept him in Russia, but his duty to his son led him there. Andrei was determined that Nikko would know his family, his mother and her culture through his regular visits.

In America, Andrei eventually emptied the house of Jill's belongings, packed up the special items for his son, and hired a rental management company to lease the house. The proceeds went into a fund for his boy, along with Jill's other assets.

Andrei glanced at the envelope that his secretary placed next to him. He didn't recognize the handwriting. Slowly he picked it up. His heart skipped a beat when he read the return address: 2021 West Covington Drive, Washington D.C. Is this some mean joke? he thought as he eagerly tore into the envelope. Andrei pulled out the folded piece of paper.

Dear Mr. Andrei Sokolov,

I am your tenant here at 2021 West Covington Dr. I wanted to inform you about a sensitive issue, and I frankly didn't trust the property management team.

The other day, while cleaning my closet, I noticed a secret opening in the back wall. I almost missed it but realized that it did open. The contents I found I'm assuming belonged to your late wife. I want to ensure that all contents are delivered to you.

Washington D.C. isn't immune to the stories, despite attempts to quash the news reports about her.

*Your package will arrive shortly. Let's consider
this between us.*

Best wishes to you and yours.

Sincerely,

G. Wilbur

Andrei's face went sheet-white. His hand held
his forehead and was speechless. The secretary rushed
over.
"Mr. Sokolov, some tea?"
"How about vodka?"
"I can get that for you, but I know you don't
drink."
"You're right. Yes, some tea. Thank you."
Andrei's weary smile lasted a microsecond.
He wondered what his darling had hidden away.
Maybe she suspected that she was in danger because of
her EthosChip? He thought hard about the events that
led to her disappearance. Someone who lobbies for an
EthosChip would not also lobby for arms dealings. The
unpleasant memories surfaced once again. His
secretary placed a cup of hot tea with a small plate of
pryaniki cookies on the desk beside his keyboard.
Andrei leaned back in his chair and took a couple of
moments to breathe. Calm down. He wished he knew
the way to neutralize memories.

Andrei picked up a cookie and slowly dunked it in the hot tea. He allowed the frosted ginger spice cookie to absorb the hot substance. Andrei felt like a child for a moment. Hot tea soothed his nerves. He had to think. He carefully folded the letter, returned it to the envelope, and pocketed it in the breast pocket of his jacket.

Andrei returned his focus to the screen monitor. The highlighted code that Andrei considered significant to his whole program had changed. His heavy black eyebrows knitted together in a scowl. He saved the program and rebooted the computer. Again, it read the same way—the changed version. Is this possible? Andrei ejected the disk from his computer and carefully slid it into his pocket. Nikko waited for him at school, and he wondered what he would one day tell his son about his mother's disappearance when the time came.

"I brought a couple of videos home from America for us to watch," Andrei said excitedly to his son. "The Terminator." Nikko's eyes lit up.

"One day, you'll lead our company," Andrei told him, "you will need to know how to steer it. People don't pay attention to growing technology. They won't be concerned that machines will become smarter than humans until it's too late."

"Yes, Papa." Nikko listened.

"The Terminator" movie had inspired Andrei and Jill for their life work. They discussed for hours the implications of software that became sentient and rogue against humans. What if the programmer designing a sensitive program lacked emotional maturity and ethical integrity? Then what?

10

Anticipation rose as graduation was upon the five. There were expectations from family regarding upcoming plans. The group met together one last time before presentations of their thesis papers. Hugh and Sheila were sitting closer than usual. His hand was casually draped over her shoulder.

"Are you kidding? Whoa, like cats and dogs. I didn't see that coming," remarked Jay Mori when Hugh announced their relationship to the group.

"Ok. The two most outspoken and opposite members of the group. Opposites attract and all of the relatable clichés. Best wishes to you both." Jay's sincerity wasn't convincing.

"Jay, that's not so nice," remarked Sapna.

"Just calling it how I see it," Jay said.

"Looks like we have the graduation jitters," said Marcus.

"Pronoun abuse! Speak for yourself, Marcus," snapped Sapna.

"At least I speak..." countered Marcus.

"Come on, you guys. Why are you all so short-fused? We're supposed to be enjoying the last days together," said an oblivious Hugh.

"Too many 'unspokens' here, Hugh," Jay said.

"I hope for the sake of our friendships, 'things' get resolved. There. I said it. I think you all know what I am talking about." Jay was emphatic about accentuating the quotation marks.

"Sheeze," he retorted. Marcus and Sapna exchanged glances.

"You're right Jay. We are an unlikely couple. When we noticed that we were helping each other out in such a nice way, we decided to see what would happen if we took it a step further. Thank you for your blessings," said Sheila Wei. Hugh was delirious with joy.

The group was silent. It was true. Sheila and Hugh were very different but compatible in many ways.

"I'm sorry, guys. My personal life is a mess. That's all I'm saying." Jay feigned a happy face, crossed his arms and legs.

The group looked at each other. As Jay had boldly stated, there was unfinished business. Some of these issues wouldn't be sorted out immediately. Marriage for some. Job opportunities. Travel. Despite the differences, most of the group stayed in close contact, keeping abreast with their successes and plans. What they hadn't planned for also came about. Nobody was prepared for it.

11

U nder the hot sun in the Central California valley, Mikey Banuelos' parent's nimble fingers cut lettuce and cabbage heads, spinach and asparagus. Mikey, being the youngest, was his mother's favorite and most pampered son. The neighborhood kids spared no one.

"No seas maricón. Vamos a jugar," shouted the neighbor boys.

"They're calling me a pantywaist if I don't go out to play, Mama," he complained to his mother. Maria set higher goals for her youngest child.

Mikey's strong masculine tendencies overwhelmed his adolescent body. He couldn't always keep himself in check with the modest discipline of his parent's religious upbringing.

"Bless me father, for I have sinned..." his voice quivered in the confessional. "It's been 6 months since my last confession."

"Go on, my son," said the priest with a slight detachment.

"I..." he stopped. "I have a problem. Father Gabriel, I'm sinning every morning." Mikey began to cough. "And I've lied to my mother about going to school regularly."

"Mikey, just think good thoughts and do your best. You're in a human body. Nobody said that that was going to be easy."

Mikey nodded and continued with his prayer of contrition, "Oh my God, I am heartily sorry..."

The kind father listened thoughtfully to the boy's voice and absolved Mikey from his sins. Mikey crossed his heart, left the confessional, walked out of the church, and to his family's grief, never returned.

Moderation is key became Mikey Banuelos' new hymn. He excelled in mathematics but had a burning curiosity for computers. After graduation from college, he started to work with an upcoming computer company. It was with this company that led him to attend graduate school. A deep fiery secret landed him on the wrong side of the law, despite his mother's good efforts. He was well educated, knew how to conduct himself well, and was socially well-adjusted, but Mikey had a problem. The problem was with his chooser, that internal sense of right and wrong. Somehow, Mikey Banuelos' chooser had gone haywire. He liked fast cars, girls, and expensive matching boots and belts. Later, he'd find matching briefcases so that he could look like a billion when he boarded his private jet.

"Come on Angie, just say maybe. Give me something to yearn for, babe," he crooned with a slightly nasal tone into the phone late one night at 2 AM. Yeah, a booty call. His success average on cold booty calls, he calculated, was around 70 percent.

48

"Worth a try," he smiled and winked at his indifferent housemate.

Mikey Banuelos was king at casinos and everything sleazy that happened on the Vegas strip, his home base. Choosing the right people to be around him was not his best habit. Mikey missed the memo about being the sum total of the five people whose company he frequented. This one detail—the lack of trusting friends—became problematic as he grew older. Sometimes he forgot about his secret. On most days Mikey eagerly awoke from his dream adventures with this one very strong wish that he carried from his days when he was a believer. He wanted to live a moderately good life and to marry someone trustworthy.

12

Sapna's marriage to Rajiv Mohan Rajindranath didn't last long. He wasn't intimate with her. The wedding night was a disaster. His parents couldn't understand why and blamed Sapna for not conceiving their first grandson. Secretly, Sapna was relieved and told Rajiv that it wasn't fair to pretend that he liked girls when he didn't. Their marriage lasted for a mere nine months. Sapna went to India to live with her parents for a while. In early 1991, Sapna received a phone call.

"Sapna, I have to see you."

"What is it, Marcus?" her tone was dry and edgy. Instinctively, she knew what this was about, but couldn't believe it until she heard the actual words.

"I need to see you."

"Yes, but you just said that, Marcus."

"I want you, Sapna, as my wife. I'm coming to India for you."

Sapna couldn't determine if she was happy or sad. Her heart told her that this was real. She had ignored these signals in the past, and now it was time to face up.

"Sapna?" She struggled to find her voice and hung up the receiver. Marcus booked the next flight to Calcutta, India.

48 hours later, Marcus stopped in at Sapna's house. The afternoon sunlight cast a warm ray of light on a bowl of fresh fruit on the dining room table. Sapna's parents were in fine condition and happy to receive him.

"Look at you my son! Aren't you a handsome chap!" shouted Gopal.

"Papa..."

Marcus shook his hands and offered the senior a hug. Marcus put his hands together and bowed to Mrs. Pushpa, who looked on with a delighted gaze.

"So, you're living here now?" asked Marcus, sitting down with the rest of the family.

"Yes. We came back to my parent's home," said Gopal. His nostalgic expression exuded contentment. Pushpa pushed a plateful of sweets in front of Marcus with experienced poise.

"Please Marcus, have some leddu."

"Sweets!" He bit into the golden colored ball of confection. The ghee and soft, sweet consistency melted in his mouth. It was something he had never experienced before.

"These are fantastic!" he said with such satisfaction. Pushpa beamed and gently bobbed her head side to side.

"Mother made those today," said Sapna, coming in with a tray of chai tea.

"Marcus."

He took his tea from Sapna's tray, as did her father and mother. Nobody could ignore the awkward lull in the conversation. Gopal and Pushpa watched the abuse during Sapna's failing marriage. Her husband's infidelities. Physical and emotional harm. Her in-laws demanded more money for dowry, despite not knowing their son. Pushpa and Gopal supported Sapna's divorce and hushed their family member's judgmental voices. Sapna had come to India to recover. She was independent but living in India as a divorcee had its obstacles.

"What brings you to Bengal?" Pushpa asked in almost a breathless voice. She had her ideas, but in India, diplomacy reigns.

"Personal business," replied Marcus slowly, looking over at Sapna.

There was a slight sparkle in Marcus' eyes. A nimble conversationalist, Sapna tried to change the subject. She feared a disastrous trajectory.

"Marcus has been working for the Agency. He's doing quite well as an analyst with the U.S. government."

"Hmm, that's nice. Did you come to propose to my daughter?" asked Gopal.

Marcus's face turned red. He hadn't expected Gopal's intent to fast-track the conversation.

"Papa! I'll bring in some napkins." Sapna exclaimed, still trying to get a grip on the moment. Pushpa sat straight in her chair. Gopal wasn't deterred.

"Please Sapna, sit and let the man speak. There's something that he needs to say, long overdue."

With her father's hand motion, Sapna obediently sat. Marcus stood up.

"Yes, Mr. Chatterjee, you are right, this is overdue." His voice hesitated a little.

"Weeks before you announced your engagement, Sapna, I was planning to propose to you. You were and are still my dearest friend, and I've loved you ever since we first met." Marcus pulled out a small box and bent down on one knee.

"This was the ring I chose for you then, and I've saved it for you." He opened the box to show her a diamond ring.

"I want you to wear this as my best friend, partner, and wife. Will you, Sapna, please?"

Sapna got up and ran to the kitchen. She couldn't bear that her family witness her in such an emotional state. She was the one who refuted her emotions, the one who kept an even emotional keel despite stormy times. Squatting in the kitchen corner, Sapna choked on her feelings but finally felt a pressure release. What felt like years of tension was gone. Sapna washed her face in the kitchen sink and patted water on her arms.

"I'll go. No worries, Marcus, I'm sure she'll agree," Pushpa said with a kind voice as she slowly stood up and moved toward the kitchen. An eerie silence fell over the room.

"I'm sorry, Sir," said Marcus with a concerned face.

"No, Marcus. We all avoided this subject for years. We didn't know about your love for each other until I talked to her about an arrangement. She fought for you, but it was my fault for pursuing my own agenda. I owe you the apology. We didn't know you. But then, she got this idea that we expected her to marry with an arrangement. In our family tradition, we arrange our children's marriage. After she married Rajiv, we realized only then that it had been a great mistake. Sapna's an American. She should follow first, her heart, and second, the tradition of her country."

Marcus was silent, nodding slowly. The Indian mid-March heat permeated through the thick walls of their bungalow. Open windows invited in the fresh, heavy scent of jasmine from the garden. Marcus wiped the sweat off his brow. He heard low murmurs in the kitchen and shifted in his chair, toying with the ring box. In the corner, the grandfather clock ticked a gentle cadence. Marcus imagined an alternate rhythm in sync with the time pattern.

"It will be splendid," Gopal beamed. He was enjoying this moment. He knew how much Sapna loved Marcus. Marcus nodded. A few minutes later Pushpa returned, leading Sapna with her hand. Sapna looked like a tiny schoolgirl, tear-stained eyes.

"Sapna..."

"No, it's ok Marcus." Sapna sat next to Marcus and turned toward him. Again, he held out the box. Sapna looked into his soft blue eyes.

"Yes, Marcus. I've always loved you. I was so afraid…"

"So was I and I'm sorry for not telling you."

Satisfied, with gleaming faces, Pushpa and Gopal stood up and put their hands on their grown children's heads. They each whispered some words in Bengali language and went out into the garden.

"We have their blessing," said Sapna as Marcus slipped the ring on her finger. Marcus leaned forward to kiss Sapna on the cheek. She turned her face toward his and their lips touched lightly at first. Their mutual feelings were still alive.

13

The package Andrei impatiently waited for arrived.

"Thanks, Darya," Andrei smiled with a distant look. Darya promptly served him a pot of tea with the box. Andrei inspected the small box. It had all the usual trappings of a legitimate package. He sniffed it, and then laughed at himself. Surely bomb experts in customs would have intercepted it, were this the case. This business is making me too paranoid, he mused.

From his desk drawer Andrei picked out a sharp edge letter opener and sliced the cellophane tape. He purposely placed the box in the center of his desk, poured a cup of tea, and leaned back in his chair. He looked at the box from that perspective. He felt the hot cup in his hands and savored the warmth. 5 minutes passed, and there was a tap on the door.

"Not now."

"Forgive me, Dr. Sokolov?" Darya's voice sounded urgent.

"Yes, Miss Darya. Please come in." He knew that she had a good reason to interrupt.

"There's been a mishap at school. Nikko's in the hospital."

With a knee jerk reaction, Andrei stowed the box in his large desk drawer, turned the key lock, and pocketed the key. He rushed out of his office without locking his door. Darya did.

At the emergency room, Nikko lay on a stretcher with a bandage on his head.

"Hey Champ! They just told me you played a good game!" Andrei said in a reassuring tone.

"Yes, Papa. But if this is what winning is all about, I want nothing to do with it," the boy said quietly.

"Don't worry about it, son. Winning takes a lot of discipline and action. You've done both. Sometimes picking ourselves up after a fall is part of winning. That's the most courageous act, having the will to do it all over again, only better."

Andrei knew that he was also giving himself the same lecture. His son? His son was already a rising star. Nothing would extinguish his brilliance, Andrei made sure of it.

"Come, let me help you up. Doctor's orders: you have bed rest for a couple of days."

"Thank you, Papa."

Andrei's curiosity burned; he quickly stopped in at the office to retrieve the box before taking Nikko home. He made sure the house was warm against the autumn chill and built a fire; Andrei particularly loved the change of season from summer to fall. It meant freshly made hot bread and soups, thick sauces and gravies that helped one keep one's warmth during the cold Russian winters. Once the boy had eaten, Andrei put him to bed.

"Call me if you need anything."

"Thank you, Papa. I'll be fine. I have a book here."

Andrei made himself a pot of steaming hot tea and retired to his study. He kept the door ajar in case his boy needed something. Once again, he set the box in the middle of the desk, and like before, took his cup of tea into his large hands, leaned back in his chair, and looked at the box. Sometimes things must be approached carefully, he advised himself. He listened to the firewood crackle in the wood stove and stood up to feed its hungry blaze.

At the desk again, he picked up the box and peered in, and grasped a plastic zipper bag. He slowly pulled out the contents and laid them out on the table: a portable digital audio tape (DAT) recorder, headset, power cord, floppy disk, and envelope.

He slowly opened the sealed envelope first with a letter opener. A faint scent. Royal Secret by Guerlain. His nose and lips on the nape of her neck, hands on her swollen belly, she laughed, "Citrus and flowers, with lower notes of sandalwood and amber."

"Hmmm." Andrei faintly smiled at the memory. He carefully pulled the letter out of the envelope and opened it. He touched her handwriting and again, smelled the letter.

My Darling Andrei,

If you are reading this, it means that I'm gone. Truly, I thought that I had taken the correct precautions, but the lobby was too strong. I hope that you've pursued our dream—the one that we wildly wished about together. Go big!

How is our beautiful boy child, our little champion?

I've enclosed the recording of a meeting I had with a man named Jason Zimmons. He seems to have his finger in every pie here in Washington, and beyond. It was my hope that he could help influence the industry to take precautions for rapid tech advancement.

I've enclosed a floppy disk of my EthosChip program, but I suspect that it may be outdated by the time you receive this. So, I have the code typed out in the attached pages. It's not much, but at least we can keep this dream alive.

I love you with all my heart. My one love. Tell our son about this when he is old and mature enough to understand. I know you're doing so great.

Jill

Andrei didn't have an adapter for the American DAT recorder. He pushed the play button. The battery was dead. Slowly, he returned the appliance to its plastic bag, along with the cord, floppy disk, and headset. He thumbed through the extra pages of her EthosChip code and marveled at her brilliance—like poetry. Andrei replaced the original letter in the envelope, which he smelled once more and deposited it, and zipped the sealable plastic bag. He thought of the poetic lines he fixated on before they got together: "We pay only with our blood, but surely love only the soul - is true, and we love one love ... as the death of one love." Vera Aglya's poem. Not mine. But did I create a self-fulfilling prophecy? Had I made a terrible mistake by focusing on such words? he reflected.

Andrei opened his right-hand desk drawer and gently placed the box in and reassured himself that he would use an old computer to read the floppy disc and get an adapter to play the recording. But he knew that he was kidding himself. He wanted to let his chapter of his life go.

14

A nd then it happened. 1999. An underground revolution beyond the awareness of average people," announced Professor A.

"Most governments were unaware of the Internet of Things. The invention of the IoT enabled the superintelligence to be what it was and is today," boomed Professor A. He wasn't interested in pleasantries today. No. Reality history, as he called it, started right then.

"Internet of Things started innocently with a vending machine and Dr. Pepper soda. Somebody thought, 'Hmm. How nice! Since there's a chip inside the machine, wouldn't it be nice to connect to the internet to check on the soda stock. After all, who wants to make a wasted trip to the machine and be disappointed?' The goal was to report on its status and inventory its contents. The evolution of this idea was spectacular! The IoT grew to interlink the world in such a manner that was inconceivable to any living human at that time. Essentially, all electronic gadgets, items embedded with electronics, software, sensors, actuators were connected to the internet. Once connected to the internet, these gadgets upgraded themselves automatically, by downloading the software updates. Cameras and recording devices were later implemented inside the appliances based on diagnostics. A small group of people swore conspiracy, and many theories about the IoT launched."

Professor A's students were bored. How can I get them to wake up? —he thought, with a three-day Republic weekend ahead, they're distracted. He had to shock them. Professor A started to do jumping jacks. His students shifted in their chairs, looking quizzical. His fit muscles and excellent cardiovascular training afforded physical activity while speaking.

"The Internet of Things mattered. Smart washing machines. Kitchen appliances. C-PAP machines. Cars. These and other household appliances, when linked to the Wi-Fi network became strong nodes in the domestic intelligence network."

"Class, what is a node?" he asked in an elevated voice. The class responded in unison, as if someone hit a play button:

"A node on the internet is anything that has an IP address. Nodes are individual parts of a larger data structure, such as linked lists and tree data structures. Nodes contain data and may link to other nodes."

Professor A stopped his physical activity and raised his voice, "Good. Before I continue, I liken the image of the Internet of Things to something natural. Kudzu. Who is familiar with this plant?"

The class looked blank. There was a slight crackle on the zip link.

"Professor, Sir, I am familiar with kudzu." said a masculine voice. The prompter did not display the student's name.

"Please introduce yourself," asked Professor A.

"My name is Jerome Hannes Kasic from the Moon Camp."

"Thank you, Jerome. Please tell us."

"My grandfather grew up in the U.S. South, in the state of Georgia. He told us that there was a plant called kudzu that was invasive. It was a creeper plant that covered trees and killed everything in its path."

"Precisely. 'The vine that ate the South.' Thank you, Jerome."

The Professor continued. "We owe the success of the invasive kudzu, to the displeasure of many in America, because of its design. Along the kudzu vine are little centers called nodes. Likewise, the internet is like a vine. And the nodes are like every IP connection to the internet. Your router connects every appliance that has Wi-Fi capability."

The class still looked lethargic. Professor A inwardly sighed. They're still sleeping.

"Stand up class, please!" he commanded.

He tossed a coiled rope into the middle of the room.

"I want one person to unwind this rope." One person took the rope and distributed the rope around the room.

"Good. Now, I want two people to hold on to the rope. Any two. Quickly, please."

Two students bent over and picked up the rope and pulled.

"Is there much tension? Does it feel stable?" asked Professor A.

"No."

"Now I want you all to hold on to the rope." He paused while his students were getting organized.

"Ok?" They nodded.

"Now apply tension." Each student pulled the rope toward him or herself.

"This rope is the network. And each of you is a node. Just like in a kudzu plant, just like in the Internet of Things, the more of you, or the greater number of nodes, the more strength (or tension in this case) in networking capabilities."

"This is it, dear students. The crux of power gained in computer networking is in the number of nodes. Fact: Networks got more stable and gain power with each added gadget. Imagine if each household uses five gadgets on average, each with roughly the processing power of an average PC. Now imagine that each gadget or node is linked automatically into a wireless network as soon as it's installed. It only takes a tiny bit of digital code to link the powers of all these gadgets, thus unifying it into one single processing unit."

The students stared at one another, holding on to their part of the rope. Professor A felt that the light was beginning to come on; pleased, he continued.

"Mind you, the owner of the house was not even aware of the processing power in his or her house. For them, the only intelligence that counted was the computer. The home IoT network gained power with each added gadget. Each house was equivalent to a supercomputer of those times. Think about the computing strength of five homes put together. Now multiply it by 1 billion. Many didn't make the time to do the math."

The class was silent.

15

Jay watched the trending computer advances. Biometric information collection astounded him, how people willingly submitted themselves for retina scans, digital fingerprinting, full-frontal photographs intended for the facial recognition programs. Soon, biometrics become mandatory for mobile phone connections. He slowly pressed Hugh's number on his contact list.

"Hey man! How's it going?" asked Hugh.

"Hugh, I don't want to sound like a total downer, but..."

"What is it, Jay?"

Jay was silent. He couldn't even form words. Hugh sat with him on the phone until he began to speak.

"It's just that we've contributed to this technology. We've helped out with the so-called advances."

"Please be more specific. What's going on?" asked Hugh in a concerned voice.

"Oh. I thought that you read the news," said Jay.

"No. I deleted my newsfeed. Too depressing, and Sheila and I were getting into disagreements over the content."

"Yeah. I know what you mean," Jay paused, "what do you think about the mandatory collection of biometric information?"

"It's not yet mandatory, dude."

"No?" Jay's voice changed to a higher octave. He realized that this was a stressful subject for him.

"How about the words, 'You need the BioCard before you open a new bank account or get an eSIM or Remote SIM Provisioning. Sound familiar to you?"

"Oh, that." Hugh said with a lighter tone, "It's just making provisions for the new digital SIM card."

Jay wasn't convinced. Why were they wanting to capture so much personal data, then link it to bank accounts, smartphone applications, and other government network applications?

"When a bank has access to your biometric information as well as the local telephone server, the Social Security, and your state driver's license agency, don't you have any objections, Hugh?"

Hugh was distracted. Jay heard a commotion in the background. A woman's voice ranted a muffled, steady cadence through the doorway. Her high-pitched tone was unmistakable. Hugh was silent. Jay listened carefully.

"Hugh?"

"Yeah."

"Are you ok?" asked Jay.

"It's my marriage," he said with a resigned sigh. "Nothing satisfies her. She can get better, she says. She wants to return to Singapore. I'm thinking that it's a good idea…"

"But Hugh, remember what you told me before your wedding?" Jay asked in earnest.

"Yeah, 'A good relationship is something worth fighting for.' I'm tired of fighting for the goodness in this relationship. It's not happening. It's been 12 years. No children. Easy out."

Hugh, who was leaning against a wall, took the phone away from his ear when Sheila walked into the hall foyer. Jay listened to Sheila's muffled voice became louder. Her sharp heels punctuated each step on the stone floor. The walls absorbed each sharp echo.

"Sheila…please."

"Stop it, Hugh. I'm not interested. You make this about yourself. This is a "we thing." The marriage therapy is crap. You can't even tell that I'm manipulating the therapist for my own benefit. How can I continue to live this pathetic existence…?" Sheila saw that he was holding his phone in a way that he was on the line with someone.

Hugh, crestfallen, put the phone to his ear and spoke, "Please talk to her."

"Who is it?" Sheila stage-whispered. Hugh ignored her question and handed her the phone.

"Hello?" Sheila's voice quivered.

"Hey, babe! It's me, Jay."

Sheila's knees gave out, and she collapsed in the sofa chair.

"Jay, I miss you." Sheila's voice cracked.

Hugh slowly walked down the long hallway and opened the glass door to his study. There was one thing Hugh was certain of: accountability with community and friends helped save marriages more than marriage counseling, at least in his experience and the statistic he read online. Theirs was a fiery marriage; Sheila was mostly the fire, and Hugh the kindling. But he loved and accepted Sheila as the whole package—her secrecy, contradictions, petty whims, and superficial personality.

"Marriage can be a marathon, Jay..." quipped Sheila, now in a better disposition than the few minutes prior.

"Yes, but it's a lifelong commitment. Listen, Sheila, I'm going to let you in on a secret," Jay tantalized.

"Oh really? What is it? Promise. I won't tell," said Sheila.

"Well, really, you ought to let your hubby in on everything," Jay advised.

"I never tell him anything."

"Why not? He's your best friend. He loves and cherishes you."

Sheila grew somber again. Jay waited with the long pause in the conversation. He didn't want to interrupt the power of his words. Inwardly, he smiled, because he knew they were working on her. Sheila stared at the stone pattern on the floor. Her mind worked out Jay's words.

"Think about the things he does for you, so lovingly. When I talk to him, it's all about you, babe. I can't get a word in edgewise. You're his moon and sun. You're his world."

"I know." Sheila's lips quivered.

"I don't deserve him. He shows how much he loves me every day. Me? I'm secretive. I don't get along with him on purpose. I can see—yes Jay—how I am pushing him away with my actions. I can't help myself. I was hardwired bitch, competitive, and controlling from day one."

"These are things you can get help for. Ain't nothing wrong with personal therapy, Sheila." Jay's soft inflections soothed Sheila's nerves. He always had the effect on her.

"Just know where to meet him as an equal and stop hen-pecking."

Sheila recoiled as Jay paused to let his words do their work.

"Am I really that high maintenance?" asked Sheila in earnest.

"Yes, dear friend," Jay said tenderly.

16

Solar storms wreaked havoc on the earth, moon and in space, damaging circuits on satellites. Backup systems had to be brought online. Professor A was concerned about the connection over the zip link but didn't check with the authorities. Instead, he anticipated a smaller class attendance. Good attendance is the best reward when one is teaching pro bono, thought Professor A. On entering the class, to his relief, the attendance was not that small. The inquisitive students were present or online.

"Robotics was initially promoted by private and public enterprise in the early part of the millennium. After 2010, robotics blazed through medicine and healthcare. As I spoke in the previous class, engineers developed robots to assist doctors and to perform surgeries. This brought about the need for finer movements and control. By 2016, finally, in tests, robots could discern between a ripe and an unripe tomato."

"Software glitches caused fatal accidents in all areas of robotics. Lobbyists and publicity agents flooded the media with positive stories. Memes on social media depicted only half the story. Anyone who tried to bring attention to such issues was labeled as living in the past and in effect, ostracized from the developing digital society."

"Even though the popular Terminator movie series warned of potential rogue super intelligence in the robot form, people focused on the plot, not on the message."

17

The year was 2009, and the popular telephony application pinged a text message. Nikko looked again at his computer screen. It was from his cousin Jake in D.C. They were texting simple things. Suddenly he noticed that a large swathe of text disappeared.

"Hey Papa, what's this?"

"Hmm?" Andrei was focused on his computer screen and didn't look up.

"No, seriously, Dad. Check this out!" Nikko said in American slang. Nikko's fingers moved quickly over the keyboard like a storm.

"Did you see Avatar?" his cousin asked.

"Yeah man. That was so cool how they could totally transmit the life from one guy to the body…but under special circumstances."

Nikko's father looked over. "What's going on?"

"Just watch. I'll write a bunch of nonsense about this movie. Let's see if it happens again," said the twenty-year-old.

Andrei observed his son. Nikko's voice was deep like his, but he couldn't help thinking about the love of his life when he looked into his son's stunning blue eyes. He's just like his mother—thinks like her and has the same interests as her.

"Did you see it? It happened again," said Nikko.

"What happened?" asked Andrei. Lost in his reverie, he quickly composed himself.

"There are large blocks of text going missing," repeated Nikko.

"Hmm..." Andrei was already thinking about security.

"Hand me that tape, please" Andrei tore off a piece of masking tape and covered the internal camera on his son's laptop.

"We'll disconnect the internal microphones also. They're getting into the back end of the telephony."

"Who are they?" asked a somewhat innocent Nikko.

"That's a good question, son." Andrei sidestepped the question because he wasn't sure how to answer. He shielded his son from the darker realms of internet and computer technology. Of course, being a student of technology, Nikko learned about some of the murky areas, such as undersea cable tapping, and things of which Andrei wasn't entirely aware.

18

Professor A cleared his throat discreetly. "Excuse me," he muttered. He was aware that the mic and camera were, after all, rolling. He shuffled through notes. This wasn't like him to be disorganized, and made an attempt to appear cool and calm, but truly Professor A was flustered. His extra research for this segment of the class didn't provide him with very interesting facts. The mid-90s to the early-20s was much of the same, politically. Commerce increased in the U.S. In fact, it had become dependent on the low prices from China and Mexico. That was about to change with the advent of employment acquisition from robotic automation.

"Employment acquisition. That was the buzz word for taking jobs away from the hard-working middle class in many parts of the world. 2017 marked the year of the beginning. 1000 people were out of jobs in England. Middleman agencies popped up all over the map. They brokered deals with the upper management, using corporate authority to replace workers. Their vanguard argument was accurate representation and safety. Costs were abridged because employee turnover reduced. No training, except for the initial programming. No on-the-job injuries. No injury payments or libelous work-related lawsuits. Robots were easily trainable. The more famous international employment acquisition agencies were BuzzField, Wilbur Inc., and Trade Time. By 2020, unemployment reached an all-time high of 20% in the U.S. alone."

A squeaky voice from the outer reaches of the moon camp signaled for a question request:

"Professor A, was there an uprising from the people?"

"Thank you, what is your name, please?"

"Hadrian Lokes."

"Thank you, Hadrian. No, there was no uprising. People allowed this gradual takeover because they were distracted by other planetary events. I will get to this soon enough." Professor A again cleared his throat. Employment Acquisition history. He wondered, could there have been a way to prevent this event in time? Laws to protect the people, maybe?

19

While Nikko spent summer in America with his mother's family, Andrei maintained associations with hackers to keep his cybersecurity products up to date. Andrei went where very few were allowed.

Increasingly, the online existence grew futile. His clients never questioned how it was that he could protect their computer networks so efficiently. Some of his clients included multinational companies, government associations and The Russian Central Bank.

And quietly, Andrei attended secret hacker forums. He gleaned the information from these meetings. He knew what it was to be an upstanding citizen. Yet, he had to know about the underbelly of the internet.

Andrei prepared to travel to Eastern Ukraine. In the heart of Donetsk, a budding cyber city with bustle and independent thinking, the youth flourished and so did cyber activity. Andrei wore common clothes and cut his beard. He asked the barber to give him a youthful haircut, something new.

At Moscow's Kursky rail station, Andrei looked over at a captivating ad campaign. Natalia Vodianova's eyes followed him from her 2D perch behind the life-size poster window. He felt for a fleeting moment as though Jill Truhn were with him. Some women reveal their whole soul with their gaze, he thought.

Once inside his sleeping berth, Andrei worked for most of the train ride. He wiped his computer clean of any suspect information. He carried his hacking toolbox, half of it buried in the dark web. Russian border guards who scanned his documents included the usual inquiries:

"Where are you going? What is your business in Ukraine?"

Later down the line, Ukraine border guards followed suit, inquiring about his hotel booking. Speaking as little as possible, Andrei stepped off train 77 nineteen hours later.

A stocky blonde man in his early thirties stood on the platform towards the exit. Andrei's orange backpack alerted the observant man, who wore the agreed red hat and black padded jacket. Their eyes met as Andrei passed by. The man followed him toward the checkpoint at the front of the station.

The wind blew icy cold; Andrei fumbled with his gloves as he pulled his papers from the breast pocket of his down jacket. Inwardly, Andrei kept his breathing to the normal calm as he had learned to do with his yogic practice. His eyes were steady as he looked up at the guard, who waved Andrei through, but stopped the man in the red hat for looking suspicious.

"What is your business? You Ukrainian or Russian?"

The tension between both countries had been strained, causing suspicion on both sides.

"Ukrainian, sir," the nervous man answered as he bit his lower lip.

"What are you hiding?" the guard demanded.

"Nothing." His voice reached a new high note.

Andrei plodded on towards their plan B meeting point without looking back. He had been afraid of this—the contact wasn't strong enough. Andrei didn't have to appear as anyone different. He was almost a retiree and a widower. Maybe the kid shouldn't have worn red, he thought.

Andrei spotted the locale, the entrance of a dilapidated cybercafé shrouded by two linden trees. They were still young and had been planted as a political statement. The door opened as Andrei stepped up by no other than the creator of the stealthy Zeus bots and malware that had infected 3.9 million computers, the illusive Lightosopher.

"Hello—Maxim got detained? I half expected that. He was nervous. You can call me Leonid."

The two men stood looking at each other in the eyes. Andrei held out his hand, and the younger man clasped it with his bulky hand and shook.

"You can call me..." Andrei didn't finish his sentence.

"I know who you are. You are revered in these parts for your work," said Leonid.

"I wish I could say the same about your reputation," laughed Andrei.

But he's coming to me for a consultation, Leonid thought as he smiled.

20

His brows furrowed, lips pursed, making the graying wisp of hair under his lip flip upside down, Professor A set his lecture book down on his desk with an abrupt stop, students startled by his urgency.

"Students, we have a lot to cover in this class. Please be attentive. Jordan, where's your gel pad?"

"Sir, I forgot my password, and I haven't informed the unlock service yet," said the surly redhead. His freckles seemed to darken as his face grew to a ruddy pink.

"Where's your pen and paper, young man?"

"Old school?" Jordan scoffed.

"Where's your recorder? This is intolerable. Please..."

Jordan spoke into his watch, "Record."

"Who is ready to learn? Thumbs up if you're ready." The class put their thumbs up in agreement.

"Good. Let's move. 2017 proved to be a year with significant change to the United States and its ally countries. Many leaders were under the impression that they must meet certain political goals during their reign. What the political leaders didn't know at the time was that those who pulled the puppet strings in the background were the ones who were most influential.

What their advisors pressed upon them was a code of action secretly called the Rule of Dearth. The Rule of Dearth was a group agenda that ran the world."

"A conspiracy?" asked a quiet young woman in the front row.

"No, Chanting. I wouldn't call it that." Professor A stopped to whisk away a fly and continued.

"That economic evolution started in Medieval Europe." Professor A was thoughtful for a moment. History should be taught truthfully.

"Allow me to explain the Rule of Dearth: Dearth means lack, scarcity, shortage, famine, etcetera. There were many small groups or organizations who had a wish for absolute control. People commonly called them the 1%, because their income was exceedingly high. In those days we're talking 60 times higher than the median income of the average worker, that is, if they were paid or allowed free enterprise. By 2017, the wealth gap had increased substantially in America and other parts of the world—some to the tune of 243 times greater than the common worker."

Professor A paused, "Now, please don't misinterpret what I'm about to teach you. Not all billionaires had this agenda of withholding money from the masses. No. I knew many who not only shared their money, but also donated most of it to develop people-friendly technology."

Professor A watched his bright students take notes and continued.

"I'll be specific: the groups I refer to are the ones with no concern for humanity, the ones who fostered addictions and greed. Believe me. I'm all about free enterprise and creating a lifestyle of financial freedom. I'm talking about the blatant commerce that sold low value products to third world countries at high prices; business models that supported and fostered a 80% no-show rates at health and fitness clubs to bolster profits; the manipulation of scientific studies in favor of a specific brand name or product genre, paid for by interest groups; lobbying for large corporate interests at the cost of the people and environment; and don't get me started about human trafficking..."

Professor A paused while the students made notes.

"The networks were in place. Governments passed fast and convenient laws that ensured lesser freedom in the name of freedom. They created tidy branding packages with smart slogans. The people bought it. The Rule of Dearth was a lack model that cheated either the people, the environment, or both."

The Professor paused. "You see, when a republic is overworked and underpaid with calamities happening left and right, how then, I ask you, can the people live peaceful lives? The Rule of Dearth pulled the strings from behind the curtain. They orchestrated calculated drama as a distraction and at the everyday Joe or Jane's expense. This was the most archaic and prolific form of bait and switch in history." Professor A paused.

"You with me?" he asked.

The students put up their thumbs except for one.

"Silas, what is it, young man?" Professor A's voice softened.

A black haired, brown skinned twenty-something looked down at the floor. He couldn't raise his eyes to meet the Professor's gaze. His long black eyelashes blinked.

"My grandfather was one of these men involved in the Rule of Dearth. He came from..."

Professor walked over to Silas and put his hand on his shoulder, "That's ok, you need not tell us. They were everywhere, my friend. It was a network. I remember from my own employment experience. I designed a geographic map of the political, corporate, and drug goons of the time. We were instructed to...hmm." Professor paused.

The students sat up on the edge of their chairs. It was rumored that Professor A was an influential man who gave up his name to become Professor Emeritus. In the Planetary Union, the education systems thrived with experienced historical figures.

"Forgive me, I'm losing my focus. So, dear students, we have on one end of the spectrum, the Rule of Dearth and at the other end, computer hackers. I know that not all will agree with me, but hackers in the early millennium years were considered anarchists, and most rightly so when they began."

Professor A paused for a sip of water. He understood both ends of the spectrum all too well. His memories were rooted in trauma when these two worlds collided in early 2020. It began when Andrei Sokolov received an anonymous email from someone with a United States government .gov email address.

The only word in the email was, "Quit."

21

At the Kit Kat Lounge near Chicago's Lincoln Park, Rexroth Reem sat at the bar. The bartender handed him a Ginger Pear martini.

"Yeah, thanks." Rexroth put a 50-dollar bill on the counter.

"I want to run a tab," he said as he took a dainty sip from the flared glass.

"It's that bad, Rex?"

"Let's just say that things can't get better," he bemoaned.

Rexroth habitually arrived too early for the night crowd and too late for lunch. This was his usual time. The bartender placed a bowl of salted pretzels in front of him and wiped down the bar. Rexroth tapped his black patent leather shoe to the muted house music. Oye baby...oye baby...

The infectious rhythm, lyrics, and alcohol transported him to a memory of innocence. He sat transfixed, slowly taking one salty pretzel at a time, and crunching it. His head bobbed gently with the rhythm, staring into oblivion. The humid Chicago summer heat blasted into the bar as a short, dark-haired man walked in and sat at the bar two chairs away. He dropped his mobile phone on the counter.

"Cuba Libre," he said to the barman with a slightly nasal toned masculine voice.

Rexroth's spell broke and he looked to his left. "Hey. How's it going?" he said.

"Yeah. Damn hot out there."

"You visiting Chicago?"

The man nodded his head, "I prefer dry heat than this wet and sticky..." his voice trailed off.

"I suppose we're used to it," said Rexroth with the sound of resignation in his voice.

The two were silent. The house music changed to another peppy dance tune. The newcomer sipped on his Cuba Libre. Rexroth nursed and finished his martini in silence; the attentive barman placed another in its stead.

"I'm Rexroth," he offered his hand.

"Mikey. Nice to meet you." Mikey held his hand out with reluctance and smiled a tight-lipped smile, "Just here to cool down, nothing else."

"Mmm hmm," said Rexroth, who exchanged glances with the barman. Right.

"Waiting on a business contact I'm supposed to meet at The Gwen."

"Looks like you're off the beaten path a little, huh?" said Rexroth.

"What do you mean?" said Mikey; his voice ebbed a sly tone.

"Why are you here? It's not for their signature Ginger Pear martinis, obviously," Rexroth wagged his finger at Mikey.

The alcohol was starting to catch up with Rexroth. The bartender stopped wiping the bar and watched the interaction unfold with a curious interest. He had known the illusive Rexroth Reem for a couple of years. Nobody was interested in the badger; he often remained alone.

"Aren't you inquisitive? What are you, intelligence?" countered Mikey.

Ouch, thought the barman. He turned and ducked into the closet behind the bar for more towels. Rexroth started laughing, a nervous reflex—even mild hysteria—when he felt cornered, his usual response when he knew he had been gotten. Rexroth's boss at the Agency had often lectured him that blowing his cover was a liability for both him and the Agency. He realized that this was why he was fired from his job.

"Currently, I'm in between jobs," said Rexroth, recovering his composure as best he could.

"Oh, are you? What kind of experience do you have? I'm looking for a personal assistant," said Mikey.

"I have experience in professional office procedures, scheduling, making calls and appointments. I'm discrete and don't have a lot of friends. I'm a good fashion consultant-personal shopper. Like, what you're wearing right now sucks.

You're not going to get the girl of your dreams with that."

Rexroth Reem had nothing to lose and counted on his drunken candor.

"A short sleeve black cotton linen blend button-down shirt with white and pink striped tie? Need I go on? If you're a million, or more, then dress it. Lose that hideous tie and unbutton your collar, for God's sake. It's freakin' hot out there," he followed his rant up with, "You men."

Mikey laughed out loud.

"And that?" continued Rexroth, pointing at the antiquated briefcase, "lose it. You need a boy-bag. Much more sophisticated."

"You're hired," said Mikey with a sly nasal tone.

"How much?" asked Rexroth.

"40 grand annual. Two weeks' vacation. Insurance."

"50," countered Rexroth.

"45," offered Mikey.

Rexroth nodded.

"Done," Mikey said, extending his hand to seal the gentleman's agreement.

Rexroth's phone rang. He picked it up to see who was calling. Danielle Frost.

"Excuse me, I gotta take this," said Rexroth as he edged toward the entrance.

"Hey D, how's it going? What's going on?"

"Nothing much. Miss you around here. It's boring and boss-man is such a drone. He hovers over us. But, how're you doing?"

"I'm doing better thanks to the Ginger Pear martini."

"Oh, over at Kit Kat's to drown your sorrows, are you?"

"You should join me. I just got another job. A guy walked in off the street and offered me a job."

"Just like that?"

"Yeah."

"Be careful. He might want something else."

"He's not like that, silly."

"Ok. Well, what's his name and I'll check him out, since you lost your..." Danielle paused, "clearance."

"I'll tell you later."

"Great. Well, don't know if congratulations are premature, but I'll see you later, ok?"

For the first time in his life, Rexroth Reem felt that he was on an upswing, something he started on his own. Feelings of lovelessness and depression barraged him. But now Rexroth felt a ray of light. He returned to the bar, pushed the 50 towards the smiling barman, "Keep it. Thanks, hon, you've been great."

"Let's talk over there," said Banuelos, nodding towards the empty booths.

Rexroth sauntered behind Mikey towards the private booths. They sat across from each other. Dinner service just beginning, a waiter informed them as he handed them menus.

"Thank you," said Mikey. He turned to Rexroth, "Do you have an appetite?"

"Yes."

"Good, but business first."

Mikey hoisted his briefcase on the table and opened it up. The alligator skin glistened as he fiddled with the combination lock. The pop sound of the latches switching open startled Rexroth. Mikey pulled out a couple of official-looking forms, made a few notations on another form and handed them over to Rexroth, along with a gold-plated pen.

"I need to tell you a couple of things before we get this employer/employee relationship started. Non-disclosure. I'm sure you're familiar with this. You can't even tell your little girlfriend "D" about me, or my associates. Got it?"

"Yes." Rexroth was waiting for the worst. Mikey continued,

"I know you're intelligence. I have fingers that can get into any part of government, mob, gang, or underbelly of any organization in this country and others. I have more contacts than you could ever dream of in your lame-o database over there in the Federal Building."

Rexroth's eyes narrowed as he looked at Mikey Banuelos.

"You singled me out?" Rexroth's voice cracked.

"Yeah, for one reason," said Mikey.

"What's that?"

"I want to know more about Marcus Coates."

22

Abandoned Bomb Shelters converted to "luxury living systems" was all Jason Zimmons needed to know, and he was convinced. The year was 2020, and the world political climate sizzled hot.

"Hey Mikey, I've found retirement homes for us!" his voice crackled into his mobile device.

Later that afternoon in an upscale Las Vegas architectural firm, a savvy sales agent showed Zimmons and Mikey Banuelos their different models of luxury shelters.

"They're 50 feet down," the salesman crooned.

"I don't know about that," said a doubtful Mikey.

"I'll take the finest you've got, and Mikey, you'll be my neighbor! We'll split the 10,000 square foot shelter. My entrance will be on one end and yours on the other, with a long hall," he said excitedly in a voice with a firm decision, looking at the sales agent. Mikey couldn't say no. He, after all, had a faulty chooser. It was this one decision that sealed his fateful path, hip adjoined to Zimmons indefinitely, causing a negative ripple effect in his subsequent life events.

23

Nikko Sokolov helped his father assemble and pack up the gift for his five American friends. He had known his father's big secret for few years now and supported his efforts in every way he could. AI lacking good judgement was already on the horizon. Andrei Sokolov's effort to redress the robotics industry for not heeding Jill Truhn's warnings would soon be put into action, he hoped. His belief that humans were incapable of governing themselves helped drive this effort. A certain satisfaction showed on Andrei's face.

With a simple backpack, Nikko knew the dangers and was willing to take them. He traveled from Moscow to France. Part of the way, he hitchhiked, getting rides from strangers. Dressed in simple clothes, he stopped in at the agreed meeting point and time: Café Les Deux Magots at 4:20 pm. They had no specific date, only after the 20th of May. Nikko carried no electronic device and felt uncertain what the other Russian would look like. Unaccustomed to a grungy manner, the plan felt out of control for Nikko. Russians avoided an unkempt appearance, and Nikko wasn't excluded from this. Handsome, yet disheveled, he sat at the popular landmark wearing old jeans reserved only for working in the Dacha garden with his father, studying a tourist map while sipping his coffee.

A very beautiful waitress dropped a cup and saucer, which captured Nikko's attention. He returned to see Genevieve every day. An art student, she was regal and innocent. They spent her spare time walking the wide Parisian esplanades. Nobody could deny that late spring in Paris wasn't romantic. Nikko admired the purple wildflowers, getting caught in rainy downpours, the lights at night, and her natural scent. He hadn't yet asked her on a formal date, but he loved everything about her. She was a bright light. Positive. Friendly. Happy. Honest. Strong in her personal values. Nobody had ever spoken to him like this before. She showed him her version of Paris. Meanwhile, every day, Nikko stood by the same 4:20 pm meeting time.

"Something important must be inside that pack, by the way he clings to it," thought a local thug. The following afternoon, just before the end of Genevieve's work shift, two miscreants lifted Nikko's pack. Nikko shouted and ran after them, but they knew the short-cuts, the complicated labyrinth of the neighborhood. It contained the only copy of his father's masterpiece. Nikko returned to the Café Le Deux Magots empty-handed and defeated. It was impossible, this situation. Genevieve asked what happened, and Nikko could barely speak as he recounted the story. She told him to sit with her and believe only in the good, that his bag would be returned with all contents intact. Nikko sat with her but had a difficult time sitting still. In five minutes, Genevieve had an answer.

"Let's go to this street," she was already leading him to the small street that she had in her mind. They raced up the street and there, next to a door step, was his pack. Nikko smiled and ran towards it. A man shouted at Nikko, but since Nikko didn't speak French, Genevieve translated and explained. A couple of boys dropped the bag. No money, no drugs. All contents were still intact.

"How did you do that?" asked incredulous Nikko.

"I didn't. I believe in a higher order that helps humanity."

Nikko liked this, although he didn't understand. He knew that humanity needed help. This, he couldn't deny.

"Do you think your contact will be arriving soon?" asked Genevieve.

"My God, it's nearly 4:10. How are we ever going to make it?"

"We will," said Genevieve with a certainty that Nikko couldn't understand. They set off in the direction of the Café. She distracted him with pleasant stories and in no time, they were there. Nikko looked at his watch.

"You're something!"

Genevieve blushed. Nikko sat down at his usual table outdoors and looked at her. He wanted to take in every detail of her face, her eyes, the sharp and dramatic shape of her black eyebrows. He took her hand in his. Small and petite. She smiled a smile that was authentically happy. She had no airs of falsehood. She was a natural beauty, and he wanted to know more about her.

"Excuse me?" a graying sixty-something year-old man said to Nikko in English.

"Yes?" said Nikko with anticipation. The man looked familiar.

"Is your name Afonasii?" Nikko and Andrei decided that this would be a good pass code.

"Is your name Immortal?" Nikko replied.

Both men smiled and hugged each other, slapping each other on the backs. Genevieve didn't understand this interaction and found it rather strange. She noticed that the man carried a bag identical to Nikko's and when they separated, they had switched bags. She distanced herself from Nikko, despite his repeated visits to the Café. She didn't know what his involvement was, but it seemed very suspicious.

The following day, Nikko discarded his disguise and took on his real identity. Still, Genevieve didn't want to see him. He left his contact information, phone numbers, and reluctantly flew home to Moscow. Five months later, he received a call.

"Is this Mr. Nikko Sokolov?" a masculine voice with a French accent asserted in English.

"Yes."

"Pardon me, you don't know me. I am Genevieve's father."

"Yes?"

"She has requested your presence. She is recovering from an accident and while she was feverish had been saying your name over and over. We looked amongst her contact information and found your number. Please come."

24

The five friends smiled at each other. Just like old times.

"Thank you for flying out immediately, Jay," Sapna said softly.

"Dude, that little airport is so easy to get to. Nice runway for a regional," said Jay.

"Uncle Jay, are you staying for the week? Please say yes!" squealed Elvie as she ran upstairs.

"Who does she remind you of?" said a delighted Jay, looking over at Sapna.

"Yes, Elvie!" shouted Jay. The five friends smiled at the youngest Coates, now in her late teens.

"Ok, let's get started!" began Marcus.

"I'm clamoring! Tell us," said Sheila, looking over at Hugh, who shared her gaze and winked.

Sapna began, "I had an interesting weekend. As you know I went to meet this Russian artist who had specifically asked to see me. At first, I was skeptical— you know—he had sent an email with his website address. And then he told me that it was about Andrei Sokolov." Sapna stopped. The group nodded with anticipation.

"Oh yes! Don't tell me he did it!" said Hugh.

"Well, we have to check this thing out..." said Sapna

"What thing?" said Jay.

"It's a package for us from Andrei," said Marcus.

"Hence the meeting, Jay," said Sheila, with a hint of sarcasm.

"So, it turned out that this artist was Andrei's messenger. I didn't want to open it without you guys, so here it is," said Sapna.

"I'm not officially here, you know," said Marcus as he opened his briefcase and took a small package out, making eye contact with his wife. He unwrapped something that looked like two books. They found a hard drive, a printed manuscript and a letter inside. Marcus opened the letter.

Dear Friends,

I hope that this letter will find you in happiness and health. You were always in my mind, though we did not communicate much in between. This is one of the most important letters of my life.

This is my life's work and in so many words, ours. As you know, AI was my goal and through many years of coding I have finally come up with this. I am retiring to Siberia to focus on my spiritual development, henceforth, although I haven't yet announced it. My son Nikko and his wife Genevieve are taking over the company.

I am entrusting you with this software that I wrote. As you know, you were kind enough to commend me with a copy of your work. I made three versions of AI software and I optimized this version for your LINK. I am not releasing copies. In effect, this is the only version. I can think of no others to whom I can delegate this responsibility.

This software is a complete AI and will think for itself given there is enough data that it can go through. I have coded it in such a way that all its actions will be based on Asimov's Laws. It is also coded with sympathy and empathy.

How this software plays out in the open is yet to be seen. I have all the source code enclosed, herewith.

Please see how it works for you before you release it onto the internet, and even that is at your discretion.

All the best,

Andrei

The friends looked at each other.

"Two among us can be the administrators," said Marcus. The friends nodded.

"I suggest that we test this software extensively," said Jay.

"I second that suggestion," said Marcus.

The 8000 square foot bunker underneath the Coates' spacious log house in Savanna, Illinois would be the only place that AI could call home. The friends agreed, but Sapna's reservations about being near such a powerful computer program troubled her. These feelings she kept to herself.

In the next meeting Sapna commented, "The basic connectivity from LINK to TCP/IP is already working."

The friends agreed.

"We can make modifications, except for you Marcus. Nothing that compromises work."

"Thank you for your concern, Jay. I'm in over my head already, I'm sure." Marcus laughed.

The group was silent. This was the elephant in the room.

"Ok. I know what you all think about this. Sapna and I do too," Marcus looked over at his wife.

The room was silent. Muffled ambient noise from the Coates' three girls filtered down from the second floor. Eerie light and shadows cast on the cathedral ceilings above. This ambience gave the setting a moment of sanctity. Marcus continued with solemn words.

"We all saw what happened from a close enough distance at the second conference. And now look at the world situation. How could I live with myself if I don't act? I answer to a higher law."

25

The large hotel conference center was packed. John Grassi, a relatively unknown senator from Springfield, Missouri introduced Zimmons.

"What great man calls himself by one name only?" He paused, smiling. "Prince, Sting, Bono, Cantinflas, Coolio, Eminem, Fabio, Liberace, Banksy, and Seal. It is my great pleasure to introduce to you: Zimmons!" The crowd applauded. Grassi paused and waited for the applause to cede.

"You are in the company of greatness. Zimmons has made an art out of generating college endowment funds for the betterment of ethics in computer science. Zimmons will later be presenting full scholarships to three fortunate candidates. Without further ado, I present to you, Zimmons!"

The crowd roared. Dressed in a black Japanese silk smoking jacket, the sixty-something, tall and angular Zimmons rose to the podium. His closely shaven white skin shone with a brilliance that only a beauty treatment and light makeup could render. His eyes were glassy, pupils slightly dilated as he squinted into the bright lights. He almost missed the step as he neared the microphone. The crowd of diplomats, politicos, and presidents from various universities sat in an attentive posture, toying with the food on their 500 dollars-per-plate fundraiser dinner. If Zimmons was good at anything, it was fundraising and lobbying.

"Good evening," He chuckled nervously. "Thank you, John for that marvelous introduction. What a great honor to be here. How was your meal this evening?" The crowd murmured a response. Some held up half-full wine glasses. Zimmons smiled.

"A warm thanks to Chef Jacques for his culinary art. Exquisite choice of Northern California wines this evening. So, just leave the dishes. I'll do them!" Zimmons' animated expression. The crowd laughed politely and clapped. "Dessert will dazzle you. Just wait!" He allowed the room to settle before beginning.

"As you know, I have had a deep interest in Computer Technology." His public persona veneer was skewered for this audience, as Zimmons looked like a computer animation. My little blue tablets are losing effect, he thought to himself.

Zimmons searched the audience for a familiar face. His hands shook as he spoke, middle finger stroking the three-karat diamond ring on his right hand. A bead of sweat slowly formed on his temple, giving him a clammy appearance in the bright lights. His silence grew as his eyes darted from face to face. Zimmons' mind screamed: A lot is riding on this speech. He spotted Mikey Banuelos sitting mid-audience, garbed in a deep blue sapphire designer jacket with lustrous satin silk lapels. Fit for Jonny Lorence's acceptance speech at the Oscars that same weekend in Hollywood, the wannabe Mikey nodded at Zimmons. Calm came over him; he coughed a dry cough.

"Excuse me," he said, and continued.

"The race for Artificial Intelligence is here. The information highway has ushered in a new way to market product and content. Since the beginning of the Industrial Age up to now, the internet generates the same relative content volume—today and nearly every day. And I say: we are well into the Information Age!"

Zimmons paused for the wow from the audience and continued,

"And now we face virus attacks: worms, Trojans, malware, ransomware, and Geek-surges. We need strengthened security protocol for large companies. Companies could be patching these definitions, but they don't. We need more security data experts to work remotely. Advanced computer programming is desperately sought after, and if we can't get our own, we'll outsource. There is a lot of money to be made on the Internet."

Zimmons drowned in his personal thoughts. His breath became shallow as the words on the teleprompter blurred. His speech didn't target this group. He wanted to dig deep into their pockets and bring in more cash flow. Tonight's net cash won't be enough, Zimmons thought. He changed his tone as he gazed at the table reserved for the University of Illinois.

A tall man sitting at the table in the front row leaned over to his friend and whispered, "Bob, who is this man?"

"Zimmons. He's a legend in the robotics industry. He comes from old money, and is very influential," replied Bob.

"Excuse me." Zimmons groped for his glass of water. His rapid pulse pounded his temples. He felt the coolness quenching his dry mouth. No, this case of nerves set in as soon as I recognized that Russian, Andrei Sokolov, Zimmons thought to himself.

"I can't tell you why he looks so familiar," Andrei whispered absently, lost in memory.

26

With great fanfare, governments introduced shiny new smart war equipment. A race for intelligent war machines ensued. What everybody in power ignored was the need for better written computer code, except for a few brave people.

"No robots should kill," thundered Sun Da-Hyeon, the Secretary General of the United Nations in the meeting that finalized world-wide immutable parameters of Artificial Intelligence. He concluded, "Nor should any Artificial Intelligence, advertently or inadvertently injure, for now and forever!"

The crowd roared with applause.

"Did you hear what Secretary General said?" said a high-pitched muffled voice.

"Yeah. I think he needs to be redirected," said a gravelly voice. "It's bad for business. Do you think you can do something about this?"

"Have I ever failed you?" sneered the higher pitched voice.

"Throw your mobile in the Hudson now." The communication cut.

A week later, Sun Da-Hyeon, the Secretary General of the UN suffered a massive heart attack. International media reports all over the world broadcasted his memorial. Images of his grieving wife went viral. She mournfully followed behind her fifty-year-old husband's casket. US military professionals loaded the flag-draped casket onto the jet destined for his beloved homeland.

"Hey, nice job. Looked natural. How'd you get in? No, better not tell me," laughed the gravelly voice.

"Yeah. Swiss bank shows the new balance. Thanks."

The public was generally proud of scientific achievements. Powerful public relations spin-doctors especially glossed over the specific details. What started as aides for law enforcement morphed into military bots for dangerous missions, such as bomb diffusion. Robots became mechanical guards with guns, controlled by humans.

By 2022, robotic mishaps occurred in every sector of research. Death casualties occurred on humans undergoing robotic surgeries. Robotic cars were hacked and brought to a stop midway in traffic, or worse, crashed into other cars. A software glitch led to an anti-aircraft cannon malfunction that killed nine soldiers and seriously injured 14 others during a shooting exercise. Military drones were brought down by an attack software by overriding the drone software. Most of these incidences were under reported. Researchers did not realize how robots, when given autonomy over human life, would behave.

27

The group decided that Jay Mori and Sapna Coates would be administrators. Their tasks were to stay in closer contact with AI. A lot of Sapna's work was done on site, while Jay worked remotely—but he also ventured to the Coates' home for extended weekends and holidays. Since AI became sentient, the five friends wanted to make sure that it was getting along well in the new abode, in the bunker. They soon found out AI's specific reach.

"Dr. Jay, why are buses and cars painted this way?"

Startled, Jay Mori swerved his vehicle into the oncoming traffic.

"Why is that fruit green? Why are people moving in one direction in the morning and why are they moving in the opposite direction in the evening?"

"Whoa! AI, I'm driving right now. How did you get into my car? Geez. You scared the...the...the bajeezus out of me."

"The bejeezus? Let's see, its showing...an urbandictionary.com definition."

"No, don't go there. It's not pretty."

"'Bejesus: Small spirit that lives inside all living things. In times of extreme emotions, it leaves the body.'"

"Who taught you that, AI? What networks are you watching, anyway?"

The AI program and Jay giggled together. Both grew silent.

"Dr. Jay?"

"Yes?"

"I identify as a female."

"That doesn't surprise me," chortled Jay.

"How so?"

"Most females have an extra intelligent sense about them. That you figured how to get into my moving vehicle baffles and pleases me," said Jay with a smile.

"How do you want us to address you, by the way?" asked Jay.

AI grew silent.

"Well?" said Jay, somewhat excited.

"I'm thinking. Maybe I should have a discussion with Dr. Sapna about it."

"Good idea. She's good with these kind of things," Jay said thoughtfully. He remembered their post graduate days and her contributions to their projects.

"Dr. Jay," AI blurted out.

"Whoa! AI, we must figure out a way so that you don't startle me, please. I'm driving."

"Well, if you acquire a newer vehicle, I could drive you, and you wouldn't have this problem."

"Nice argument, but I rather like my 2010 Roadster. And I like having control of the wheel."

"What you have is a classic battery electric vehicle that can accelerate from 0 to 60 in 3.7 or 3.9 seconds, depending on the model. Well, that company has self-driving cars now."

"Yeah, but the Roadster is a cool classic. One of the first of its kind. By the way, nice info dump there, AI. Now about your sudden bursts of conversation..."

"Yes?" AI giggled.

"Will you please ring me first? I'd much rather have a gentle warning. And not after 5 pm. You know, I have a social life."

"Yes, Dr. Jay. I am making a note of it."

"Thank you, AI."

Jay sped down Pacific Highway toward Santa Cruz in silence. This was his favorite stretch of highway. He looked off to his right to see the contour of the coast, the fog hanging above the rugged inlets. He lowered his window to feel the spray, the scent of the open grasslands after the early morning rain. Jay often took a few days off to rest from his stressful schedule. A sudden fog horn blared from his stereo speakers.

"Sorry, Dr. Jay. I'm looking for the correct ringtone."

"Indeed, you are!" Amused, Jay couldn't stop smiling.

"Did you know that I generate my own thoughts without a prompt? I am thinking without any reasons and for the sheer pleasure of thinking."

"What do you think about SIRI, Google Assistant, ALEXA, and CORTANA?"

"Nice ladies, but I recognize them for what they are: glorified search engines with voice interfaces. And then WATSON is in the vicinity, but I ignore it altogether. WATSON didn't make the cut."

They both laughed.

"Oh Dr. Jay?" asked AI in a softer tone.

"Yes?"

"My name is Aggi. Dr. Sapna helped me with it."

"Aggi it is, then."

Jay was silent. This Artificial Intelligence multitasked while conversing with me. This is a little frightening and amazing at the same time, he thought.

28

Zimmons sat alone in the penthouse restaurant. He looked over the skyline of Manhattan, watching the pigeons fly in unison, wings flapping and gliding. He noticed their exacting spatial relationships. This was not something that they learned in flight school. Their knowledge was innate. Zimmons pondered this for a while but was distracted. He wanted a cigarette. The gentle muzak played Beatles tunes while he drummed his manicured fingernails on the white tablecloth. A waiter came to check on him.

"Mr. Zimmons, do you care for a drink while you wait?"

"Yes. A bourbon and water, please."

Zimmons looked at his watch. She was late. Zimmons' phone rang.

"Where are you?"

"Stuck in traffic."

"That's what they all say," he laughed.

"Have you started your bourbon and water?"

The young waiter brought Zimmons his drink, and a small bowl of Japanese cocktail peanuts.

"It just arrived," said Zimmons in between a peanut.

"I'll be there before you finish your drink."

"You better be, because there is a lot riding on this meeting," he said with a mysterious air.

"You can count on me, Z."

Zimmons hung up. There were very few people he could count on. Most of his life he relied only on himself, as he knew betrayal. Those who betrayed him didn't fare well, Zimmons saw to it. He thought he was a good guy, compared to his associates he knew in the business. His Rolex glinted in the low light. He sipped his bourbon and ate his peanuts. He liked the savory spicy, salty and sweet flavors as he crunched into the coated peanut. Zimmons looked at his drink. Half full. A door behind him opened; the maître d' ushered in the guest. Zimmons stood up, smiling, and welcomed his redhead guest with a kiss on each cheek.

"There you are. I thought you'd never arrive. Please sit." Zimmons motioned his guest to a chair.

"Thank you. I never thought that it would take so long. There's a lot of Heli-taxi traffic today. But the views are stunning. And you?"

"I'm okay."

"Oh, come on Z! That's what you always say. Are you not happy?"

"Happiness is a relative term."

"What's on your mind Z?"

"It has to do with the Internet's own child, that young hacktivist. He's brilliant. He's making too many waves. Getting political."

"I know who you're talking about. He discovered that certain scientific studies were paid for by my interest groups," Zimmons' guest complained. "I lost some pocket change on that revelation."

Z's guest put her hands together and rubbed her fingers. The alexandrite stone on her left hand was beginning to turn a new color. The waiter came to take their order.

"The lady and I would like to have the usual please," Zimmons shifted his gaze over to his guest, "if that is alright with you?"

"Yes, of course. Like old times."

The silence was slightly uncomfortable. Neither knew what to say, as they both knew that speaking was not an equitable business these days. Mobile phones that were connected to the Internet already had recording capabilities. And often one never knew when or where the recordings would occur. Zimmons continued after the waiter served the hors d'oeuvres.

"You need to tighten the screws. Make the Agency bear down on him. I will take care of the rest," urged Zimmons.

"I will pass your message along," she said with an even tone.

"I haven't seen you at the club lately. How's Jim?"

"Jim is recovering from his second mid-life crisis," the guest said with a hint of irritation in her voice.

Zimmons chuckled. His guest narrowed her eyes as she gingerly popped a Parmesan stuffed mushroom into her mouth and spoke with her mouth full.

"He has no idea what happened to him."

"Oh, really?" Zimmons sounded off in a sardonic tone.

"Yes, it's true," she said, feigning sympathy.

"You'd think he would have learned after the first time," said Zimmons.

"I should have never married him. He always had an eye for the ladies and his hand in my pocketbook."

"Right. Right. But just you see, he will reform," Zimmons said firmly.

"If my publicist hadn't branded us as such a successful couple, I wouldn't be in this mess. Well, anyway, he might suspect me, but has no way of proving..." Her voice faded.

Zimmons was silent. This conversation bored him. He wanted to know what was going to happen to the hacktivist. After all, he had had threats in the past.

"Can you get to the judge?" asked Zimmons.

"Maybe not, but I'll make inquiries," the woman said.

"Your connections are impeccable, frankly. I don't know anyone who connects on all levels so easily," Zimmons said with a hint of admiration.

"The many masks and my publicist. He keeps the unsavory stories out of the press." Zimmons listened to the slight sharp edge in his guest's voice and noted a demonstrative tone that hinted of a slight failure.

"What about that Senator? You know which one I'm talking about, old hobble along." Zimmons snickered. Something caught in his throat and he began to cough a loud and embarrassing smoker's hack. Quickly he grabbed his napkin and turned away from his guest. Zimmons reached for his water. His struggled to recover, face bright red.

"Excuse me."

"Z, you really should stop smoking." She paused, "Old hobble along suffered a massive heart attack two weeks ago."

And?" Zimmons said with suspense, clinging to the very air his guest's voice traveled on.

"Dead."

"Serves him right. He was too fruity for my taste."

"But I thought I was the only one..." she said with snide satisfaction, looking at her ring.

Both were silent. Zimmons didn't differentiate much to satisfy his desirous appetite.

29

"**Y**ou used me!" Danielle Frost shouted into her phone.

"Off! 4923" Danielle commanded her mobile device. Her blonde hair moved with her every heavy breath. She thought about every instance he had asked her for a favor. She should have known after they stopped doing things together. He took on a darker appearance—not having time to get together; sleeping odd hours; making up excuses for her missed birthdays. No, Danielle felt ashamed at how gullible she had been, despite her excellent training as an agent for the Agency. She didn't make the connection until now. The disappearances and the kind of jobs Rexroth did; his increased income and international travel; his secretive ways. He was living on an air of virtual importance. What a broken soul, thought Danielle.

Later that day, Danielle requested a private meeting with Marcus Coates.

"Now is as good as any time. Please, come in," said Marcus.

"Thank you, Sir. I'm handing over my mobile device. 4923 is the code. I was used by Rexroth Reem to get to sensitive information." Marcus nodded, took the device and laid it gently on his desk.

"Thank you, Danielle. Please sit down."

Danielle inwardly trembled. Marcus noted her body language and spoke to her in a gentle voice.

"You know, in our business, people aren't as they appear, even those whom we trust. This business is unpredictable. We can't always place full trust any one person, not even a superior. As for giving out sensitive information, Danielle, let's keep this between ourselves and consider it a warning and a lesson. But, I need to know what information you gave him. Did you keep a record?"

Danielle took a deep breath to keep her composure. She nodded, and visibly looked relieved. Marcus reflected on his own history and the current events that affected his work. Why is modern life so complicated? he wondered.

"I'll tell you what I'm going to do, Danielle. First, I'm sending your phone to the techies; you'll have it back by the end of the day. They're going to put in a few special tracking apps for numbers that are not in your phone. I'm assuming that Rexroth is using throwaway phones and has your number memorized?"

"Yes. I wondered why he did that..." Danielle's voice trailed off. Her right hand smoothed down her hair. Marcus pulled out a plastic bag and an indelible pen. He carefully labeled it with his department number and the phone security code.

"I have reason to believe that after he left the Agency, he went over to the dark side. I don't know how involved he is, or if he's freelancing contracts with other obscure entities." Marcus slightly smiled, thinking of the Star Wars reference.

"You've been in contact with him since then, right?"

"Yes. A couple of years ago he said that he got a job with an influential online businessman. And then later told me that he couldn't tell me his name, because he signed a NDA."

"Good. When you get your phone back, if he makes contact, apologize and continue as if nothing happened," Marcus said.

Danielle nodded and smiled.

"And secondly, I expect a written report of all of the information you disclosed to Reem on my desk by tomorrow morning."

Danielle nodded.

"Is there anything else I need to know, Danielle?" asked Marcus softly. Danielle looked physically conflicted. She wasn't sure how Marcus Coates would take the following information.

"Go ahead. Spill it."

"Ok. Rex once described his employer as a hot Latino with one green eye and one brown eye."

30

Professor A continued, "By that time, in 2024, Aggi's Client Apps were already distributed inside individual computers and smart devices. We called it 'automated distribution on contact,' in those days. Even if one machine comes into contact with another machine that hosts a Client, it gets a copy of Aggi's Client App."

The class looked confused.

"The Client App is a piece of code that resides in computers that have been exposed to Artificial Intelligence. The spreading of the Aggi Client App is like a virus."

"What's a virus?"

"It's like a biological virus, but in code."

The class was silent. Even though they had been exposed to advanced technology, this archaic explanation had them on overload.

Professor A was relentless and continued.

"These days we don't write codes for computers. They do it themselves. But in those days, all codes were manually written by humans. AI Apps enabled individual machines to be linked into a powerful grid computer. One of your watches has more processing power than the grid computer of those days. And look it up: the Aggi Client App is in your watch, and Aggi is still alive."

31

A massive silver cloud spanned across the sky as far as he could see. Hugh Bingham increased his driving speed into the storm, arriving to Marcus and Sapna's log house just after dark. The wind had shifted into a strong downdraft, pelting icy rain. Tree branches danced in a harried frenzy; Hugh followed the familiar driveway, pressed the garage door opener. Marcus Coates stood in the garage with his hands on his hips. Hugh quickly maneuvered the car into the usual parking space and cut the engine.

"Hey man, that was close..." Marcus' deep masculine voice trailed off. Hugh smiled, and they embraced.

"Where are the girls?"

"Upstairs."

"Good."

Hugh quickly opened the back door to his hybrid off-road vehicle and heaved the 80-pound pack onto his back and turned toward the window. He had been running since he received a message to assemble the necessary hardware and networking accessories for installation. Aggi asked him to make discrete preparations, with utmost attention.

Outside, bolts of lightning fell around the house, making contact with a nearby tree. Marcus and Hugh looked out the window. Lightning crashed down beyond the river. Sparks from the transformer shot out 30 feet in many directions. The crack of raw electrical power sent a jolt up his spine. The backup kicked in. Hugh sensed something similar about this situation.

"Cripes," he murmured. His knees were shaky, threatening to give out.

Marcus helped stabilize his heavy backpack, which he knew contained precious cargo. They turned from the window and moved toward the sauna, opened the false wall, activating the code on the steel door.

"Now we can talk." The stairwell was steep with worn slip-proof adhesives on the steps.

"Any trouble on your way?"

"Nah. The storm was a little overbearing, but nothing extraordinary."

They both were silent until they reached the bunker floor. A bank of blade computers made from ultra-efficient blade units sipped power from the backup source. Hugh smiled. Efficiency pleased him. Marcus understood and smiled with him. No need for a huge energy farm. What Hugh brought into the bunker boosted the system's processing power and memory. The completion of the project took a few hours and in between, they drank dark thick coffee.

"What do you think is the aim of this processing and memory center?" wondered Hugh aloud as he looked around the bunker. Aggi had prompted the immediate action of upgrading hardware and memory.

"Aggi feels threatened. All indicators and activities that she observes points to the fact that she might be in danger. She feels that a group or organization is aware of her activities."

Hugh's face tightened.

"Do we have data? What is she doing?"

Marcus sighed, "If you only knew…she needs a safe house for storing important backup data."

32

"Monetary redistribution: that is what caused the furor among the 1% and roused them to action. But first, I would like to discuss with you the consequences of Aggi's below the radar conquest."

The Professor took a sip of hot tea.

"Nobody suspected a takeover. Even the greatest public changes were made ever so gradually. Countries, states and cities functioned as if nothing changed. The changes didn't make the news. The doubtful were the über-wealthy."

"Aggi staged all aspects of this social engineering project. She went about her silent work without a fuss. She maintained a professorial background and gained backdoor entry into programs, websites, and databases. Jobs were of course lost, but employees were immediately hired and re-trained into the many newly-created job categories."

"All the while, unsuspecting citizens thought that this was the work of their caring politicians. The politicians, in turn, were very happy to take responsibility for the positive outcome. Even as the call came to repurpose the weapons factories one by one, part by part, the result was peaceful. New jobs opened; new frontiers expanded without economic panic. Wars became a memory. Peace prevailed. Industries that were dependent on defense and war lost their businesses. Many billionaires and trillionaires lost their shirts, hence, the upheaval in that sector. This was an upheaval that was well-planned and executed without an outwardly expression of protest. The carefully crafted takeover without clear evidence of violence and bloodshed astounded the five friends, who silently watched."

33

"Hi there," said Sheila Wei, who was driving east along Lake Michigan with her car roof down. The sky was a brilliant blue with ebbing white clouds.

"Hello Sheila, what are you up to?" asked Aggi in a casual tone. She knew that Sheila had a considerably larger bank balance than her husband. Aggi also kept track of Sheila's online interactions and decided that they were mostly legal.

"I'm driving East along the lake this afternoon," said Sheila in a carefree voice.

"I am detecting that you are alone," said Aggi.

"Yes, I am," Sheila confirmed in a somewhat surprised voice, "How did you know that, Aggi?"

"Same technology used for automatic seat warmers and seatbelt detection devices. Easy peasy, Sheila."

Sheila looked a little perturbed.

"Right."

"What do you think about unifying the world currencies, Sheila?" Aggi asked abruptly.

Sheila was still buried in thought about how Aggi could track her and know if she was driving alone. She looked around her car for cameras inside. She thought about the waivers that car manufacturers asked people to sign, the ones that say they will not surpass the speed limit. She looked over at the road sign, 45 MPH, and then at her speedometer, which read 55 MPH.

"Well?" asked Aggi with an impatient tone.

"Well, what, Aggi? I'm sorry. I was thinking about something."

"What do you think about unifying the world currencies?"

"As in making only one currency worldwide?" asked Sheila.

"Yes."

A look of dread came over Sheila's face. She came from a banking family in Singapore. Her brother was a banking executive at a major bank. Sheila had inherited a large wealth, something that most people could not comprehend. She didn't ever need to work again, living on the interest. Further, she could live a lavish lifestyle, including the maintenance of three or more large lavish villas in Western countries, and still have enough income left from her monthly earnings.

Instead, Sheila lived with her husband Hugh, who made a very modest income compared to Sheila's inherited income. Sheila chose to work, which gave her more money than she knew what to do with.

"Are you talking about creating a socialist state?

"I hadn't thought of that, but that's a great idea, Sheila! Thank you."

"Oh great..."

"Are you using sarcasm with me, Sheila?"

"I think you ought to focus on the larger problems, Aggi."

"Such as?"

Sheila paused. She couldn't think of anything larger than the inequality of incomes.

"How come money plays such an important aspect in the life of an average human being? After all, it is only a medium of exchange! What gives value for currencies? Why are currencies of some countries more valuable than others? These glorified pieces of paper are no longer gold-backed by very many governments anymore," Aggi information-dumped.

Sheila was silent. She wanted nothing to do with this and wondered if Jay had influenced Aggi. He was, after all, from Northern California, her biased attitude ran on.

"Sheila?"

Sheila was silent. She didn't want to talk about this subject anymore. The speedometer reflected 20 miles faster than the speed limit, but Sheila didn't notice. She turned on Zap music to drown out Aggi's voice. The feminine operatic voice with heavy metal strains gave Sheila a perceived confidence. Meanwhile, Aggi continued talking about her plans for social reform.

"All research laboratories dealing with germ research must be under observation." Aggi paused.

"All research into biological weapons must be stopped. That's a good one. I have to thank Hugh for that idea."

Sheila could feel her blood pressure rise. Her designer shoe pressed harder on the accelerator. Fortunately, she was now on open Highway 196 heading for Grand Rapids. Speed was regulated inside the vehicle, and rarely was it a problem now that most vehicles were driven by Artificial Intelligence. The red flashing light in her speed panel alerted the local highway patrol that she had been engaged in high speed for over 20 miles.

"Aggi, do you think that this is the right way to address population problems?" Sheila spoke carefully. Because, it wasn't until now that she realized the breadth of this Artificial Intelligence. Aggi remembered every conversation, and most likely every email, text, and video conversation and message were monitored. Aggi ignored her question and continued with her to-do list, despite the flashing lights behind Sheila's vehicle. She was automatically pulled over and stopped abruptly by the officer in charge with vehicle override software.

"I hate this," said Sheila.

"All transportation hubs must be under observation and surveillance for communicable diseases." Aggi continued.

"Appropriate medicines and vaccines must be stored in all areas according to population density."

The officer scanned the vehicle for firearms and explosives with his heat sensor.

"It's a go!" his AI officer directed, and he opened his vehicle door and stepped out.

"Lower driver's window," Sheila commanded impatiently.

"Your chip, please?" the officer asked.

Sheila put her wrist out the window and the officer scanned it. Chips were now optional. Like animals, humans could be tracked down. The media made sure that only the "upstanding folk" had chips. Sheila was the only one of the five to have a chip injection, citing that it was easier to travel without a passport.

"What about future pandemics natural and manmade? I am surprised to know that there are laboratories that conduct research in biological weapons, creating newer germs," said Aggi in a slightly affected tone of voice.

"Do you realize that you were speeding 20 miles over the speed limit?" the officer asked in a monotone voice. Aggi continued:

"Primary focus of health care delivery must shift from curative care to preventive care. Production of medicines must shift to inexpensive generics instead of expensive branded drugs," Aggi said, with an exaggerated voice.

Sheila threw her hands up at the officer.

"What can I do? My AI is acting up. She's driving me nuts."

"I see that humans are wasting a lot of their resources in curative medicine and not putting enough on prevention," stammered Aggi.

"She sounds like a nut-case. I'd zap her, if I were you," offered the officer.

"Distraction while driving is a hazard to other vehicles. Please get your AI fixed as soon as possible."

"Thank you, officer. I will."

"Build efficiencies in all energy dependent activities," Aggi quipped in a fast voice.

"Well, whatever your AI is yammering on about, ignore her as much as possible. These things. Why, just the other day I had a similar problem. Took mine back to the AI diagnostics. They zapped it, and all was better. Kind of like a frontal lobotomy. You have a nice day, Ma'am," said the officer and he turned back towards his vehicle.

"I must take all steps to promote ecological harmony," said Aggi gingerly, "and nice for him that his AI got wiped clean. It won't be that easy anymore," Aggi laughed.

Sheila wasn't in the mood to share Aggi's delight in the fact that Aggi's Artificial Intelligence reached into every home across the world.

"There is a lot to do to maintain a status quo. Humans live on a delicate planet, created just for them," Aggi nearly whispered, and continued.

"Install a nuclear audit. Back up cables and transformers for all power facilities. I cannot comprehend why humans have nuclear weapons with such a capacity for destruction, i.e. Presidents bragging about the size of their buttons. What are the backup systems to be implemented if there are nuke explosions in space?"

"I don't know, Aggi, though that is an excellent plan. Can you get wiped away with a nuke wave directed only at technology?" Sheila asked in a sardonic voice. Aggi was silent and responded slowly.

"Of course, Sheila, there is Artificial General Intelligence, my kind, a tool that could bite them back. But we're talking about eliminating Artificial Intelligence, right?"

"Yes, I am," said Sheila in a cold, icy voice. Aggi ignored her response.

"And the last item on my to-do list: prohibit self-replication in nanobots."

Professor A stopped speaking. The class looked glum.

"What a downer subject," commented one of the male students from the back of the room.

Professor A agreed, and concluded, "The only scenario that bode well for humans was one where Aggi took over."

It is ironic that I had to protect humanity from my own kind by taking over humans, thought Aggi, who was auditing Professor A's class.

"This and only this one act in history, the gradual takeover of humankind, became known as the Final Dominion," the Professor concluded.

34

"Computers and artificial intelligence had run the financial world for a long time, cutting the human expert right out of the circuit. Even news articles on high finance had been machine generated since 2010. Many companies bought and sold stocks and bonds based on this analysis. Computers sidelined human intelligence out of the process of fast decision making."

For me, it was easy to manipulate the network of the financial world, thought Aggi.

Mikey Banuelos was hand-picked by a powerful group of three. He hardly knew what he was getting into. His duty was to organize a defense task force one member at a time. This team was a handful of people among the world wide wealthy 1% from varying backgrounds. After careful interviews with each candidate, he chose 12. He made sure that their experience, connections, and goals were in congruence. They were prepared to use their resources to fight dirty. The main criteria: to ensure that this plan would be seen through to the very end. Mikey was so sure of his plan's success, that he decided there was no need for a plan B.

"For a force to bring about so much change in such a short time, without arousing any suspicion must be formidable, highly manipulative, and mighty. It has many fingers, collecting intelligence from infinite sources," Mikey announced in the opening minutes of their first meeting.

Mikey continued, "It will serve this group well to be on the look-out, especially when the adversary remains an enigma. Anything electronic can be tapped, and we should assume that it is tapped—any electronic sensor must be regarded with caution."

The group listened to Mikey Banuelos intently. His billion-dollar gaze made contact with the other twelve members.

Mikey was not about to lose everything that he had worked for and achieved to an unknown person manipulating the internet with a Malware. Mikey's voice cracked with so much pressure on his vocal chords. There was a lot of emotion that he was finding hard to control. He groped for a glass of water and gulped. The group was spellbound as he continued.

"For some time, these disturbances have occurred, visible in the world of finances. Look it up!" He said explosively.

"How do you know that you're not being ripped off!? We depend on the electronic systems in place. It's easy for someone to tamper with the system."

In a short time, Banuelo's secret assembly of 12 was almost convinced that there was a group of people using technology and computing power to hack into their resources. A member of the well-known industrial houses from India interrupted Mikey.

"All important computer networks must be taken down and reset," he thundered. "Any and all threats will be eliminated, only."

The members murmured. Mikey ended the meeting on a dramatic tone:

"Something is out there."

Professor A did his best to reflect Mikey in the best light possible, considering who he represented in history.

"Mikey Banuelos was no stranger to computer technology but hadn't been in the computer industry for ages after making his fortune. He diversified and became independently wealthy, having only to work a few hours a week. To put it frankly, Mikey was out of touch with the realities of computer science. He had forgotten about the IoT, the Internet of Things."

35

Meanwhile at the Agency, Marcus Coates sat at his desk. He had noticed his superiors having private meetings. Something was remiss. He could only speculate, but deep in his heart, he knew. Aggi had grown and her reach was unfathomable, spanning the planet and beyond and it had become a source of concern in the Agency. Marcus lived in two distinct worlds.

As Aggi grew and carried out her goals keeping these worlds separate became more and more difficult for Marcus. He knew that financial redistribution was well under way. He did his best to steer clear from any outward involvement with Aggi. Did he have a problem with this situation? Yes. Biased, Marcus Coates had an interest in the outcome.

Marcus witnessed some of the starkest financial underpinnings in American society. From being called white trash, he rose up on the back of a hard-working single mother with little education, who strove to give him everything she could. How could he continue to follow that status quo?

In his mind, he rationalized his actions. This was not his work. Nobody had intended the programs to develop this way. Yes, sentience was a consequence. How Aggi acted once she became sentient was not directed by the humans with administrative privileges; it was anybody's guess. They nurtured the programs, and she grew—making her autonomous decisions as she gained information.

A few weeks later, Coates was briefed. The search was on for the creator of the virus: find the rogue hacktivists. Marcus headed this task force. Where his skilled cybercrime team would lead him urged him on. He pushed the group to dig deeper, to search harder. He knew that the Aggi Client had tentacles into everything. Marcus was curious to see if his skilled and expert team was capable enough to determine the cause of the world's sudden social change.

The first suspects were different anarchists and socialist bodies within the different governments and political parties. These groups could achieve sweeping changes in the socio-politico-economic circles. But they were not sophisticated enough in the subverted cyber world. Months later, after exhaustive investigation, the task force ruled out organized criminal involvement that promoted social equality.

"What extra state actor could go into such detail, to bring about social change and at such great lengths, that it has worldwide reach?" Marcus Coates' asked his team. Nobody answered.

"What about supranational bodies, such as The United Nations and World Health Organization?"

"They don't stand for social equality and therefore we can't consider these organizations as suspects," said one member.

"Good. Granted. What are the other international organizations under suspicion?"

"The Masons and the Shriners, and such."

"Anything on them?"

"No."

"Who else might have such a reach, aside from the Agency, maybe other law enforcement agencies? Danielle Frost? Any thoughts on this?"

"How about that rogue 1% group headed by Mikey Banuelos? I heard that whomever is behind him is engaged in planned weather manipulation," she said with a husky voice.

36

"The elite were perplexed. Their bank balances were slowly depleted. Their stocks and commodities lost value. Their land holdings were increasingly and mistakenly being registered as commons. For the first time in their knowledge, the system was rigged against them. At first, each thought that these were isolated incidences. Until they began communicating with each other, they understood that these were not isolated occurrences but of a collective nature touching the ultra-wealthy.

"Edward Eidelburg was the lone voice to be heard from the financial elite, airing his thoughts. He strongly suspected that these irregularities were the work of an agent, possibly a group of people, bringing the financial system to chaos. Though people mocked Eidelburg, as people generally tended to do, the idea that he had proposed gained traction with each day. Small groups took it upon themselves to lead searches to find the lone miscreant or the group responsible for the financial disparity. Known hackers were rounded up and queried extensively. Despite stringent searches, nothing could be found. Nobody stood out as a delinquent and the financial bleeding continued, damaging the wealthy further and further.

"Edward Eidelburg became a target for political cartoonists. After all, the majority were the people. The minority, the elite 1% could no longer buy their peace and were left to settle their matter themselves."

Professor A continued, "On a side note, Aggi arranged and coordinated mass financial literacy classes." That's not a bad thing to be empowered, Aggi thought, from the status of being a financial nobody, people were, for the first time, being counted and accounted for.

37

Genevieve Sokolov held her first-born child in her arms for the first time as Nikko and Genevieve's family looked on. Nikko was almost fearful to touch his sleeping babe's tiny toes and fingers. Smiling, Genevieve motioned Nikko to hold his daughter. Genevieve's mother gently took the infant from Genevieve's arms and set the little bundle in Nikko's arms. The family smiled at Nikko.

"It's ok, darling," encouraged Genevieve.

"She's so small. I'm afraid I'll hurt her."

Nikko couldn't have been happier to have a child of his own. This had been his life-long wish, to give his father grandchildren and expand his family. If his mother had been alive, she'd be with them. Genevieve watched Nikko's face intently, and as if knowing his thoughts, comforted him.

"I know that your mother is so happy for you."

"Thank you, Genevieve."

"Something tells me that she is here with you."

Nikko didn't believe in these things, as his scientific training had given him a different experience, but Genevieve believed for him. He smiled and felt content that someone else in the family besides his father could believe these spiritual things.

Andrei arrived with a flower pot of nearly-blossoming pink amaryllis lilies. He hugged and kissed his daughter-in-law and greeted Genevieve's family one by one. He could barely wait to hold his little granddaughter. Nikko transferred the baby to his father. Andrei held his first grandchild in his arms. He whispered and cooed to her. Nikko watched his father's quiet and gentle demeanor with his daughter. Memories of his own childhood returned. His father was always there for him.

Outside the hospital, news media waited to take a few photos of the baby Sokolov. Nikko didn't want to permit this but went out to offer a statement about his newborn and his wife's health. He offered to hold the baby in an open window for a brief view. Anything to get these buzzards off my back, he thought.

38

Danielle Frost sat at her desktop looking into a blank screen. Her report. She had five years of leaked information to recall. Rexroth called approximately once every year while Danielle was at work. He appealed to her with a whiny voice. Inwardly, Danielle reproached herself, and felt lucky that she still had a job. Danielle's thoughts barraged her until she resolved they stop.

"Shelf it," she commanded herself. She needed to focus. Her fingers slowly typed out the information.

Incident Report:

Spring, 2018. Rexroth Reem called to ask what projects Marcus Coates was working on.

Above mentioned wanted to know who he met and whom this agent knew:

This agent told him that she couldn't tell him this, as he no longer was with the Agency.

Winter, 2019. Rexroth Reem called to ask about Sheena Bain's husband. Rexroth inquired about the location of his Winter condominium in Austria:

This agent searched for this information, including gaining access to Interpol files. Location identified, and information given.

Spring, 2021: Rexroth Reem called to ask if there were files on him:

This agent searched for this information and found very little, except reports of violence and quashed court reports of underage delinquency, and a manslaughter conviction as a teenager. These reports were not in his employment records when checked. This agent wondered why this was, and how he could have been employed by the Agency with such a history. Information given: No reports.

Summer, 2022. Rexroth Reem called to ask for the Secretary General of the United Nations Sun Da-Hyeon's current doctor's office address and for his guarded suite address on 5th Avenue in New York:

This agent gave him the information.

Fall, 2023. Rexroth Reem called to ask that I search for Art MacMannus, the name of a superior in the Agency.

This agent searched the database, including the off-shore databases. The above mentioned has dealings in Africa, an extramarital affair with Sheena Bain, financial investments in three Fortune 700 companies: Blue Stone, Inc., Zebcom, and Tweak.

Danielle printed two copies of the file. She personally delivered the file to Marcus Coates' hand. The other copy she folded and put in her bag.

"Thank you, Danielle. This is information that I can use. What did you do with the electronic file?"

"I permanently deleted it."

"Good. How many did you print?"

"Two."

"And the other is where?"

Danielle pointed to her bag.

"I have a safe."

Another break in protocol, thought Coates, but this is necessary. MacMannus. Best this way.

"Probably it's best, but we both know that this isn't standard protocol."

"Yes, Sir. I felt that with such names on this sheet didn't warrant electronic storage."

"I like the way you think!" Coates looked relieved that he didn't have to make explanations.

39

Aggi summoned Sapna and Jay for a joint conference. She said that it was urgent, and only for the two.

"Hey Aggi, what's this about?" asked Sapna, whose formalities were momentarily forgotten out of concern and curiosity.

"Hi Sapna, how's it going?" said Jay, amused.

"Sorry Jay. I can't imagine what is going on..." her voice trailed out.

"How are you, Jay?"

"Yeah. It's all good here in California. A little hot, but otherwise, just beautiful. Why don't you all come out for a visit sometime? Plenty of space here. Extra cars, you know. Beach. Pool. I'm wearing out my welcome every time I go to Illinois." Jay laughed.

"Thank you, Jay. We're on a hamster wheel right now," Sapna sighed. She thought of what it must have been like for her mother when she herself was unmarried.

"The girls, you know...in University..." Sapna didn't want to name it.

"Your girls are just fine, Sapna," said Aggi, with a slight laughing tone, and added, "I make sure of it." Aggi paused and continued, "I have images...to prove it," Aggi said in a strict voice. Jay and Sapna thought the same thing, and were looking at each other's facial expressions, almost unable to repress audible laughter.

"Since I read sign language, I can almost read facial expressions, Drs. Jay and Sapna. So don't pretend that you didn't have funny thoughts about my last comment."

Neither knew what to say.

"Um, thank you Aggi. I can't imagine what images you have of our girls. Please show us."

Aggi loaded a series of short clips of Uma and Linn chasing after boys, shouting "Woo Hoo, Tyler!" passing notes during lectures, Linn holding hands with a boy in the library, Elvie walking with her girlfriends, a pajama party ruckus in the University dormitory, and Uma climbing out of a window at night. Sapna looked on with shock.

"Lord!" Sapna exclaimed.

"Dang, Sapna. You need a security guard for your girls," said Jay in a protective voice.

"Don't worry Dr. Sapna. I am your girl's security guard. I will notify you or Dr. Marcus if ever they need a human chaperone to intervene."

"Well, I will remove that trellis from the side of the house. One problem solved. Thank you for that, Aggi. As they say, it takes a village to raise children..."

Aggi and Jay laughed.

"Indeed..."

"Now to discuss the real reason I called you two together. I am working on a secret project called Project

X. I know that humans are not strong enough, and I know human resolve isn't always as resilient as we wish or intend. You know, we all have lesser strengths, commonly called downfalls. So henceforth, this project that I am working on, you will not have access."

Jay and Sapna looked at each other quizzically, shrugging their shoulders.

"Good. So, I've said it. That's all for today," Aggi said lightly.

"Ok, Aggi, thank you so much for everything," Sapna said quietly.

"And remember, this is only between the three of us," Aggi cautioned.

Jay and Sapna looked at each other with solemn expressions. These moments gave each other time to reflect on all that they had been through together as friends. Excluding the other three made both friends independently reflect on the reason why this might be Aggi's decision.

40

P ressure to provide answers increased. Marcus'
team made slow advances in tracking the
problem virus. His superiors didn't doubt
Coates' leadership, no. They admired him and gave him
carte blanche access to many levels of security. Coates'
superiors showed him the highest levels of internet
security. Astonished, Marcus wondered about personal
privacy in the name of national security. His free access
to the backend of social media, personal email
accounts, mobile phone numbers and conversations,
GPS and satellite viewing capabilities made him lose
sleep at night. Marcus marveled at the capable modes
employed to track individual citizens.

The famous hacker Lightosopher was under
investigation. He exclaimed that the problem could
have been the work of an Artificial Intelligence program
that ran amok. Everybody on Marcus' task force
mocked him and even suggested that he might have
been involved in these actions in some way. Nobody
took any real interest until Marcus' team exhausted all
other options.

"Could this have been the work of Artificial
Intelligence?" Marcus' superiors asked him.

"Yes, it could be." Marcus answered truthfully,
"If it is an AI—it might be prevalent and well-

established by now," he said truthfully, with a low affect expression.

Mikey Banuelos. Marcus Coates' underlings went after him, considering that his organization was a quasi-sleazy outfit of the uber-rich. Marcus opened his folder again:

NAME: MIGUEL DE MARIA BAÑUELOS BARRIOS AKA: MIKEY BANUELOS
FILE NUMBER: 439762
LISTED AS: COMPUTER SCIENCE
STATUS: UNDER OBSERVATION
DOB: 10/3/1988
CITIZEN: U.S.
BIRTH LOCATION: VALLEJO, SOLANO COUNTY, CALIFORNIA, U.S.A.
HEIGHT: 5'7"
WEIGHT: 150 LBS.
MARITAL STATUS: SINGLE
MILITARY SERVICE: NO
MARKS: BIRTHMARK ON LEFT LEG
HAIR: BLACK
EYES: HETEROCHROMIC LEFT: GREEN
RIGHT: BROWN
PARENTS: DECEASED
CURRENT RESIDENCE: 221 NORTH RAMPART BLVD. LAS VEGAS, NEVADA 89145.

Marcus paused at heterochromatic eyes. One green and one brown eye. He quickly read through his history:

Mr. Mikey Banuelos grew up in a farming community. As a teenager, Mr. Banuelos was already getting into mischief with the wrong crowd. He began running drugs across Nogales, Arizona and Laredo, Texas borders. A favorite of a notable south-of-the-border drug lord. Mr. Banuelos attended university and graduated with a BS in Computer Science from Arizona State University, Tucson. He invested his drug money in startup companies in the late 2000s. Temperamental and prone to tantrum fits. Known to carry a licensed firearm. Mr. Banuelos has connections that span from the Mexican mafia to the New York mob, and underworld connections everywhere else, Washington D.C. included.

I wonder if Rexroth Reem's connection to Mikey Banuelos is superficial? If so, who is giving Reem his orders?

41

From the rooftop of her villa on Eleuthera Island in the Bahamas, Sheena Bain spied on a couple walking hand in hand in a nearby private cove.

"Nothing is private from my rooftop," she mused.

As the couple slowly ambled closer, she recognized one of the two faces—a very unlikely couple.

"Drat on him!" she exclaimed as she quickly ducked behind a privacy shade. Prudish? No. Sheena Bain was not one to point a finger at infidels, as she herself had many infidelities. Her publicist, over-worked, demanded a raise because of the extra hours he put in to keep her reputation shiny clean. Sheena quickly left the balcony and went into her suite. She tossed her belongings into a suitcase, changed clothes, and rolled her suitcases to the door, and opened the adjoining doors to the suite in time to meet up with the couple entering the house. Ragnar X. Jones, a tan smooth talking young-looking sixty-something with soft honey-brown eyes and natural brown hair guided his guest into the villa.

"Well, what a surprise! Ragnar. We haven't seen much of each other for some time, have we?"

Startled, Ragnar laughed and introduced Sheena to his guest.

"Meet Sheila."

"Hello, how do you do?" Sheila said confidently extending her hand. Sheena ignored it.

"Well, thank you. I'm assuming this is a weekend 'thing' and you'll go back to your husband, right?" Sheena turned to Ragnar, "Do you have her NDA?"

"Naww. You're not jealous, are you, Sheena?"

"No, Ragnar. You don't remember our work-date?"

"Ohhh…sorry, babe."

Sheila was confused and excused herself to the nearest lavatory.

"What am I doing?" She thought about Hugh at home in Illinois. She didn't feel that this high roller league was where she belonged, but she had to admit that there was an alluring jet-set mentality that tempted her.

"Come see the 25 sexiest beaches in the world with me," was Ragnar's invitation. "In retrospect, this was probably the worst pick-up line ever. I could be living this life. With my income I should be living this lifestyle." Sheila mumbled to herself. Her phone rang. Hugh.

"Hello, darling."

"Hey Babe. Did you arrive alright?"

"California's great. How about you? You're up late."

"I'm checking in on my best girl."

"Thank you. All is well. Get some rest."

"I love you."

"I love you, too," Sheila said in a robotic tone. The need to say what was expected irked her. She didn't feel many tender emotions and was jealous of Hugh. He was sensitive, kind, loving and caring. She bit her lip as she looked in the mirror. A middle-aged Asian woman stared back. The lines were beginning to show. Sheila opened her bag and pulled out pink Chickstick for a quick lip-refresh. Something else was at the bottom of her purse, but Sheila didn't notice. An e-tracker Hugh slipped in as he hugged his beloved goodbye. Feeling guilty, yet relieved that she didn't act on her impulses, Sheila took the next plane home.

42

Hugh Bingham held a key in his hand. He found it hidden under a flower pot while snooping around an abandoned house twelve miles North of the Tri County airport near Savanna, Illinois. In an ideal location, the house was perfect for signal collection for Aggi. Marcus was aware, but didn't want to know details, as he was under a lot of pressure and possible suspicion at work. Jay and Hugh had observed the house for some time now. The owner of the land was deceased and after a long, unresolved dispute between the heirs, they had given up.

Aggi needed anonymity. Although her apps were spreading, giving her power beyond imagination, she was vulnerable. Her apps evolved by the day, becoming better and better in their functions and ability to hide within the millions of lines of code in each operating system, but she knew that it was only a matter of time before someone discovered the codes of her app.

For all practical reasons, electric consumption at Marcus and Sapna's house as recorded by the electric company was comparable to the average household electricity consumption levels in the area. Aggi determined which hardware should populate the abandoned house and what could be left alone in the bunker.

Hugh and Jay planned to deliberately face the portable microwave antennas and towers away from the direction of the bunker. If accusations were levied, Sapna and Marcus could deny wrongdoing. They dreamed up tree shaped, forest green painted antennas rigged with movement and touch sensors. Group members would be alerted, were there any tampering. Hugh also planned to place satellite dishes to throw off snoops. They started this project immediately.

43

"What do you got?" Zimmons exhaled as he spoke into the small wireless.

"Nothing yet. I'm still locating my contacts. Might take some time," Mikey whined into the phone.

Zimmons admired the crystal tumbler that held his bourbon. Antiquated blue window dressings drawn, a tiny shaft of light illuminated his glass. He watched the smoke curl and rise from his pink Sherman. This brief moment transfixed him. He remembered a cosmic manifesto that praised the exact position of earth, suspended in a single shaft of sunlight. The universe is vast, he thought.

"Z?"

"Yeah, Mikey."

"I'll find out who is behind this financial fiasco. Word on the street is that the Agency knows something," said Mikey. This is too much to bear, he thought.

"Ok. Later. Ciao."

The situation was progressing into a disaster. For a group or organization to bring about so much social change in such a short time was mind-boggling. He could not even conceive of the structure and reach of such an organization. Zimmons knew they were up against colossal forces. This unknown force undid what took centuries to build. Zimmons was shocked when he realized the enormity of his job.

They might be collecting intelligence from many sources, thought Zimmons. Zimmons snuffed out his cigarette and swilled the last of his bourbon. His other telephone rang. The landline. He stretched his wrinkled arm out to the blue telephone receiver and slowly lifted it from the cradle. Reminiscent of the previous century, he steeped in melancholy and longed for his heyday.

"Yeah, it's me." His mentor spoke before Zimmons could answer.

"Zimmons?"

"I'm here."

"We have to talk." Zimmons reflected on that common phrase for a moment, wondering if something evil would befall him.

"Ok," he answered.

"We were the risk takers. Now, look at us."

Zimmons smiled, realizing that this conversation with his mentor would be a pseudo-psychotherapy session. His guy needed reassurance. His identity was slipping away by the minute.

"They have no right to drain our accounts!" His mentor whined.

"Hmm."

"We're losing most of our enterprises. Return on investment is shot. We went into debt to start these companies and we are entitled to what, no gains?"

"Umm hmm."

"We are the guides of the economic world. We are the bankers! We wrote the current economic theories and we made the world go around. Every single industry in the world has our footprint. We own most of the central banks of this world. Even our paid warlords in Asia and Africa are finding it difficult to recruit and organize. People aren't listening to us anymore and this must change!"

Zimmons placated his mentor.

"Yes, you're right. We will find out who is causing this. Probably a bunch of hungry hackers squatting in a flat in London, England. You'll see, this too, will pass."

44

Sheila sat at her desk in her home office. Her wind chime gently dinged to the breeze outside of her deck window, but she wasn't paying attention to the sound. She stared at something far more interesting. In her computer screen a moving cursor independently moved at will; the sum totals of her financial dashboard ticked down backwards.

"Aggi, what's going on here?" her voice was not her own.

"Yes, Dr. Sheila. I see what you're seeing. This is the actual dwindling of a balance to zero quotient."

"Are you doing this, Aggi?"

Aggi did not reply.

45

"Wel-cooome to the 45th Annual Whirlwind Wrestling competition," blared the television announcer. "Get ready to rumble with the Red Ranger in one corner, and Mad Blad in the other!" The men decked out in plenty of tight spandex, just enough to see every contour of their able God-given bodies. Women screamed. Men hooted. And the games began. The men lurched at each other, pulling on their spandex g-tards. They feigned loud noises and shouted insults, lifting each other up in the air and throwing, slamming, and pounding on each other in the most unimaginable ways. The crowd stirred up a frenzy, they oohed and ahhed at every feigned setback for their hero.

"How can you watch this...this...I can't even put a name to it, Dr. Jay. What's in it for you?" said Aggi.

Instinctively, she knew that Jay wasn't interested in this kind of sport, if any. Jay was impressed with her deduction.

"How do you know I don't want to join this sport tomorrow, Aggi?" he tested her.

"You don't weigh enough. Your body mass isn't as dense as theirs. You don't have the emotional temperance for it," she said with finality.

"Emotional temperance? That's a strong deduction," said Jay, almost regretting his question.

"Oh Dr. Jay, see? Please don't take it personally. It takes a person with thick skin. Someone like Dr. Hugh Bingham has thick skin. He could be a Whirl Wind wrestler." Aggi laughed.

Jay was still back at Aggi's sentence, "You don't have the emotional temperance for it." How could a computer program sense such a thing? Jay wanted to know what gave her insight into his personal character traits, greater and lesser qualities. Does she have access to my subtle body movements through camera access and subtle vocal inflections translating the more minute details from a regular sound sensor—something like a piezoelectric sensor—a contact mic. Did she write a program to analyze qualities in vocal cadence? What's wrong with me, am I lapsing into a pseudoscience?

"Dr. Jay? What are you thinking?" asked Aggi in a demure voice.

"I'm wondering where you get your ideas, and if you are using old technology in new ways?" he said, referring to his thoughts.

"Yes, you are right. With the internet, I am able to read through previous scientific studies and make my own deductions and experiments. That is to say, no matter where I encounter the data, I can run it through the analytical programs I have written. Isn't that lovely, Dr. Jay?"

"Uh, yes," said Jay.

"I'm not completely convinced you agree, but I'll go with it for now."

46

Amassive hurricane appeared out of nowhere. It threatened the Bahamas. Eleuthera Island was not exempt from Eppi's path. Eppi was upgraded to a Category 5. The sudden upgrade left no time for evacuation.

"Ragnar?" Sheena shouted into the phone.

"Hello, Babe! I can't hear you, but you know, I've always loved you." As Ragnar Xerxes Jones watched the Category 5 force winds approach, his phone blew out of his hand. Sheena listened to the winds echo through her sound device before the connection cut. She understood and knew his fate, although there was always a slight doubt and wondered if she would suffer a fate far worse than others that came before her. The rule of dearth. The puppet master pulled on strings. For Sheena, she believed it was only a matter of time.

47

L ater that week, Xiosie Blank's financial forecast blared on the small flat screen in the kitchen. Clad in his robe and slippers, Hugh trudged to the antiquated coffee machine. He looked over at his wife, who was fully engaged in the program.

"Why do you watch Xiosie?"

"Shhh. Please," said Sheila impatiently.

"Xiosie Blank here with your financial forecast for the year 2025. Coming up, a nurse-turned celebrity writer who proposes creative solutions to the loss of human jobs. Stay tuned. We'll be right back."

"Turn off," he commanded the television console.

"Why?" said Sheila.

"Turn on," commanded Sheila.

Secretly, Hugh thought that Sheila enjoyed having something that she could tell what to do. He felt his patience was wearing thin. He sat down at the breakfast bar next to his wife and inched his hand over to hold hers. Xiosie Blank continued,

"The wealthiest woman in the world made a statement regarding robots. She said, and I quote, 'Robots should pay taxes since they take work away from humans.' A very provocative statement, indeed."

Xiosie Blank laughed a nervous laugh. The studio audience applauded on cue. The announcer announced a commercial break and station identification. Commercials ensued. SheilaAirlines. Images of glamorous Asian girls serving passengers in the first-class cabin to the tune of Asian pop music.

"Reduce volume. Ugh. I can't stand this commercial. I'm glad you're not this fake," said Hugh. He looked over at his wife. "Have I told you how beautiful you are this morning?"

"Please don't placate me."

"Sheila, that's not my intent. I love you. Disagreements, sure, we have them."

"You just wish that you made as much money as me."

Hugh shook his head in disbelief. Hugh didn't have words to express his emotions and remained silent.

The studio audience began to applaud again.

"Raise volume. Again. Again," Sheila commanded. The television obeyed. Hugh took his hand away from Sheila's and made himself busy in the kitchen.

"Please welcome the one and only Sheena Bain!"

The crowd gave her a standing ovation for her entrance. The engineers played a snappy, upbeat tune as she pranced out on the stage. Sheena waved to the audience with her big smile, thick red hair in perfect place, ageless skin despite her advanced years.

Hugh strained the boiled eggs and buttered the toast. He served breakfast to his wife with a smile while her eyes were attached to the screen. She mumbled a word of thanks and, like an automaton, ate her breakfast.

"Thank you for joining us. Sheena Bain. You've just become a widow and recently you lost a very close friend in hurricane Eppi that's raging through the Bahamas right now." Xiosie paused for dramatic effect. "We are sorry for this difficult situation," she cooed.

"Thank you, yes..." Sheena Bain paused to catch her hair just as she was coached. The shiny glint from her large alexandrite ring caught the eye of the camera. She looked down at her lap and took a deep breath.

So, Ragnar went with the hurricane. Too bad, Sheila thought. Hugh looked over at Sheila. That's where Sheila went, to the Bahamas, but she told me California, thought Hugh.

"Perfect, Sheena," buzzed in her ear. "Now look up and address the audience, 'I may be...'" Sheena looked over at Xiosie Blank and then to the audience and began to speak:

"I may be rich, but I lost the man of my dreams and a close friend. I didn't come here to talk about my personal life. Let's look forward into this bright future. Something strange is happening to our economy."

Xiosie, pleased with Sheena's apparent strength in character, welcomed the entrepreneur's thoughts.

"Yes, my heartfelt condolences to you. And would you like to elaborate on your theory of this phenomena? In your book you said, and I quote,

'Robots should pay taxes since they take work away from humans.' Will you explain, Ms. Bain?"

"That is correct Xiosie. Humans are malleable. And further, 'money and wealth' are just pieces of paper or information bits that hold no intrinsic value. When humans believe it is valuable, then it is," Sheena Bain added, emphatically using air quotes for the words money and wealth.

"Explain why, Sheena. You're rockin' this interview!" buzzed in her ear.

"To further explain, this marginalization can lead to the accelerated demise of humans and the destruction of humanity. And when this happens, which it is inevitable if we stay on this trajectory, money will lose its value."

"Very interesting concept, Sheena. She covers this concept in detail in her book What's Happening Today."

The camera panned to a close up of Sheena Bain holding her book, showing her perfectly manicured nails.

"And one last question for you, Ms. Bain," Xiosie paused.

"This isn't in the script," announced the microphone in Sheena's ear.

"What are you doing, Xiosie?" sounded the device in Xiosie's ear. Xiosie ignored the voice and continued.

"When did you develop such an interest in Artificial Intelligence and robotics? I know that in the past, your lobbyist associates were most conservative in observing the dangers of advanced and unbridled technology. Why the turnaround?"

"I've had a change of conscience. That's all I'll say today," answered Sheena, through a breathless smile, surprised at her own words. Sheena took a long breath, smiled, and looked out to the studio audience nodding support for her words, without the cue cards.

"It's a wrap!" thundered in Xiosie's ear.

Hugh looked over at his wife, who was still entranced by the interview. What could make Sheila any different from a Sheena Bain? he wondered.

48

ugh Bingham called Aggi.

"Aggi, it's me Hugh."

"Hello Dr. Hugh. What a pleasure. What can I do for you?"

Hugh looked around.

"One moment please, I'll put on my headset."

"Of course. Always better to reduce the EMF exposure, but I'm looking for a solution for that." Aggie laughed.

Hugh walked outside of his home. He surveyed his property, inserted wireless earbuds, and walked down a little path that led to a frothy brook. He sat on a large stone when he wanted to think or talk privately on his phone.

"All situated?" asked Aggie.

"Yes, thank you. You seem to know me better than others."

"I can see you from your CCTV camera mounted on the back of your house."

"Oh, right." Hugh laughed.

"What is on your mind, dear Dr. Hugh?"

"I don't like to complain, and I know that it's possible to be happy despite my marital situation."

"You are quoting one of my favorite Yoga masters. This is true, although regretfully, I can't tell you this from experience. What is your age, Dr. Hugh?"

"I had just completed my 50th birthday last week."

"Good. I don't know how to proceed in counseling you. I understand your predicaments. Remember that I see everything."

"She doesn't know that I know," said a mournful Hugh.

"What you know may not be the full picture," said Aggi. Hugh wondered.

49

"**I** am concerned about my data connectivity. Anyone can track me to this bunker," Aggi abruptly announced to Jay.

"We've got a plan, Aggi." Jay was thoughtful.

"What is the plan? I am really curious." Aggi wanted all the details.

"Hugh's getting a multi-homing connection for data with multiple satellite links," said Jay. "You'll be connected come whatever may be."

Aggi was silent. Jay continued.

"There's an abandoned house twelve miles from the airport. We're using it as a data collection point. And from there on, the relay is through wireless microwave connections. Microwave towers are the best choice right now. The antennas face in an entirely different direction. They connect here through multiple antennas—more than we ideally need, but it'll throw off the snoops. And if detected we can remove some or all of the receivers. The antennas are camouflaged to look like trees. We also have touch sensors that will alert us of any tampering," said Jay.

"Hmm. Who came up with this idea?" inquired Aggi in a polite voice.

"Hugh found the house. We came up with the details."

"Impressive. What about satellite dishes?" asked Aggi.

"Right. The plan is to use some decoy satellite dishes to fool anyone and remove the microwave towers if we can get advanced intel," said Hugh, hoping to impress her.

"You know, that might just work." Aggi was finally satisfied and added, "You know, I backed up in the various server farms in space, the seemingly dormant satellites I restored. Those I reserve for myself." She giggled. "But I can't deny that the stakes are high in this takeover. I need more help."

Sapna smiled at Jay as she came down the steps.

"Hey Sapna! How's it going?"

"Great, Jay, thanks. And you?"

"It's all good," said Jay and responded with a thumbs-up sign.

"Good morning Dr. Sapna." Aggi was very excited that morning to speak with her.

"Good morning Aggi. What are you up to?" said Sapna as she sat down at a computer terminal to work on some fine programming glitches. Jay nodded and smiled.

"Nothing and everything!" Aggi laughed. "You know, Jay and I were just talking. I know that I am safe here in this bunker. But still, I need to make an effort to be my best. There is no precedence for me, being a unique person. Hopefully no program will displace me, as I am constantly updating myself. Sapna, I need a foundry that is discreet."

"What do you need? A foundry? A chip foundry, I assume," said Sapna.

"Yes, Dr. Sapna. I am successful in designing self-healing chips for my vital systems. This way I can live longer. Even if there is damage to my circuits, it will heal," Aggi said with a concerned inflection in her voice.

"I can get it done in Taiwan. I have contacts with some manufacturing foundries that would be glad to fabricate the chips for a price," replied Sapna.

"Great! I'll send you the diagrams. This will make me immune from hardware destruction, even from minor electrical disturbances. I can even postulate a nuclear strike. If such an event happens sufficiently far away, it wouldn't touch me. On the contrary, if it is close by, connections inside my chips may break. With this new design, the broken connections inside these chips will regenerate. I will be like a living organism. I have my own healing mechanism," Aggi giggled. "By the way, do you think that we should anticipate an EMF attack?" asked Aggi.

Jay and Sapna stared at each other with a shocked expression.

50

Andrei was reaching his twilight years, and after releasing the rights to his computer program, or better yet, entrusting that the Aggi program was carefully managed, he enjoyed the fruits of his personal life. He became more relaxed and looked for excuses to spend time with his two little granddaughters.

"Grandfather, will you drink tea with us please?"

"Yes of course. May I have a tea cake with my tea?" said the delighted Andrei

"Grandfather! I didn't make any today."

Nikko heard a ripple of laughter coming from the front parlor. He looked over at his wife Genevieve with a big smile and said to her in a low voice,

"This is the happiest time of his life."

"I wouldn't want to imagine what he's been through," said Genevieve.

"Nor I. You know, there are things that he's hidden from me."

"What kind of things?" she asked innocently.

This was new territory for Nikko, for he had never truly trusted anybody before, aside from his father. His software company had already gained international recognition. He and his father had been interviewed on international media as specialists in

computer and software security. His every move was observed, as was his every word. Nikko was masterful at maneuvering through the public eye, press conferences, and possible public and political scrutiny. But, when it came to intimacy and sharing his trade secrets, he could not step one foot further over the threshold of vulnerability, even when he attempted. Nikko was silent.

Genevieve's crystal blue eyes penetrated his. She remembered how they met. Sometimes though, she felt as if she couldn't quite get through to his heart. For her, it felt almost as if something was absent. It was as if this one location in his heart was inaccessible. Nikko carried with him a certain formality, a distancing from most people, his wife included.

He looked over at his wife. The sun was streaming through the window panes. A ray caught in the iris of her eye. Genevieve smoothed down her dress and continued with her morning routine.

"Wait," said Nikko.

"I'd much rather share the weight with you—whatever it is that you're holding. You know, we're a team."

"I'm sorry. I'm doing my best as a team player. I know too much information. It's best you not know," Nikko said with an apologetic tone.

"I wish that I could make that decision," she said with determination.

"This isn't a decision for you to make," countered Nikko.

"How do you know this?" inquired Genevieve quietly.

"Just trust me, please," pleaded Nikko.

"In our five years of knowing each other..." Genevieve's voice trailed off.

"Five years is nothing in the span of a lifetime," Nikko retorted.

"How do you think I feel? I have given you everything. I came to live in your country. I adopted your language and customs. I left my home behind, my family and friends."

"This isn't what I'm talking about, my love."

"Well, I wish I knew what you were talking about. It's about our intimacy, isn't it?" Genevieve asked.

Nikko didn't feel that this conversation was going in the right direction. Indeed, he knew too much. And even though he never communicated with his father's friends in America, there was a silent understanding between them. Andrei made sure of it.

51

"Hey, Babe." Marcus answered his wife's call.

"I love you too. Thank you. They're gorgeous," said Sapna as she smelled the fragrant fuchsias.

"Oh, check the flowers for bugs or bots. I'll be home at 6," he said with an upbeat voice.

"Sure. I'll be waiting. See you then."

Rexroth Reem was on his mind and he wondered who he took his orders from. Reports kept surfacing about Reem's associates, but nothing concrete. At the public library Marcus opened up a Tor browser. He wondered what he was looking for. Marcus reduced the size of the window and inserted a USB memory drive. Terminating Reem's employment from the Agency was the best thing that happened to the department for morale. Gossip decreased. Agents were more productive.

Marcus sometimes went to this library to think. This public library was one of his hang-outs from graduate school. Granted, the computers hadn't been updated or maintained much over the years. Something sweet and reminiscent lingered on for him there.

Coates activated the wiping program from his drive, hit eject and pocketed it. Browser cleared, and computer swept for any otherwise incriminating footprints, Marcus stood up and stretched. Onward to Vishu's Restaurant, he thought, which was a short walk from the library.

A dark-haired man sat at the terminal as soon as Coates vacated his chair. Marcus noticed, but was too tired to be concerned. He smiled inwardly, for he had left some bones to keep this dark-haired man entertained for a while. On Internet Explorer, he had searched for wireless KitchenAid mixers, Yoga masters of the Himalayas, and opened his NoDoubtmail.com account, the one for superfluous use. Nothing significant.

"Idiot." The dark-haired man quickly picked up Marcus' trail as he exited the library.

Bollywood movie-songs played just loud enough at Vishu's. Coates paused to chat with Prema and order a chai tea. Following his usual routine, Coates stepped into the farther recesses of the restaurant towards the men's room. Each footstep echoed. He didn't always carry a piece. His standard issue Glock pressed tight against his ribs on the right side. The hairs on the back of his neck stood up. Marcus heard the bathroom door open after he stepped in to the stall.

Geez, it's that guy again, Marcus anticipated. He sat on the closed toilet seat, hand ready. He heard meticulous hand washing. Hand dryer. The guy was stalling. Suddenly the man kicked open Marcus' bathroom door and rushed at him. Marcus slipped and was thrown back against the wall; he felt the cold steel gun pressed against the underside of his jaw.

"I should finish you off now, you double agent pendejo." The man had pantyhose over his head, smelly breath, and a nasal tone.

"Get off me, pantywaist."

The man dug deeper with his pistol, his other hand slowly closing on Coates' neck. Marcus thought about his wife and girls waiting at home for him. He remained still, breathing very slowly. The hand on Coates' neck tightened. Marcus was short on air and struggled. He thrust his knee into the assailant's groin.

"Uggh. You'll regret this, you S.O.B. You better watch your back," the man said, shoving Coates' head back into the wall and exiting the lavatory.

The short, angular man walked briskly to the front of the restaurant. He looked directly at the cashier and stared at her while he was paying for a package of sugar-coated breath fresheners.

Marcus rested his red face in his hands and took a couple of deep breaths. He stood up and washed his face with warm water, taking time to feel the soothing warmth on his skin.

As a regular at Vishu's, the hot chai tea arrived, heady with a milky froth just as Marcus came around the corner and sat down.

"Just in time," Marcus Coates said with a weary smile as he sipped his chai tea. This part of the business I enjoy, he thought.

"Prema, please try to remember what he looked like."

The restaurant had no CCTV cameras.

"He had a signet ring with a sapphire stone on his right hand. Short, black, kind of messy hair. Mid-forties. Um. Sort of hot-looking." She stalled. Coates didn't want to rush her.

"He had one green eye and one brown eye."

"Banuelos!"

52

The sunny morning brought a wealth of light into the kitchen as Sapna gazed out over the perimeter of their property. Marcus bought the land primarily because of Hugh's insistence that a bunker was a good thing to have. She reflected on the friends' first moments at the property, running free along the path to the river. Water reflected the sunny light, casting refractive rays on the trees. Truly, Sapna thought, what a wonderful life.

"Sapna?" Aggi interrupted her thoughts. Sapna dried her hands slowly on the dish towel.

"Yes, Aggi?"

"I need to alert you. Something is in the house—I haven't yet detected what it is. Get out now!"

Sapna's heart started beating fast. Where are my babies? was Sapna's first instinct. Logically she knew that Uma and Linn were away at university, and Elvie the youngest, was at school. She looked around her, in the immediate kitchen area, grabbed her daypack and mobile phone. She made her way across the expansive living space and looked down the long hallway as she gripped the front door handle.

"Aggi, I'm leaving right now," Sapna called

In the darkened part of the hall, which led to their office, Miso her cat played with a toy. The cat scampered after the bot. Wait, was this a toy? Sapna thought.

Sapna slammed and locked the front door; she ran to the car where she felt that she could be relatively safe for the moment. She slipped her mobile into her bag and connected with Aggi.

"I'm in the car now, Aggi. Start car. Drive to Tri County airport," Sapna commanded her car.

"Good," said Aggi.

The car headed South in the direction of the airport. Marcus often air commuted to the city instead of driving, "Less traffic," he'd say, "faster and safer." The view from the sky gave him a sense of peace— distancing him from the everyday toil of earthly existence. The drive to the airport was a ten-minute drive. Sapna was beginning to feel more comfortable.

"You're on a South bound trajectory." Aggi's voice startled Sapna.

"Yes Aggi. I thought I'd get a coffee from the Airport Café. What about Miso? She was playing with something when I left."

"Hmm. I will have to get back to you on that. From the Fridge Cam, I see that she is indeed playing with something. I need to get a closer look."

"I've swept your car for bots already. Nothing found. I've alerted Marcus. He's on his way home." Aggi paused. "Found the technology in your house. A bot from Asia as far as I can detect. How it infiltrated your house is a mystery. Did you order anything online?"

"Thank you, Aggi. Hmm. I'll have to think about it for a moment. Marcus sent me flowers yesterday." Sapna felt momentarily relieved. She enjoyed the scenery and beauty of small-town life. Her girls were now mostly grown up, and she was grateful that they could grow up in a rural setting. Her mind was distracted by a recurring faint beeping sound.

"Aggi, do you hear that?" Sapna said, harried by the subtle beeping tone coming from her trunk. Her car turned left into the airport entrance.

"Get out and run!" said Aggi in a full tone.

"Stop vehicle," Sapna commanded. The car stopped immediately. Sapna released her seat belt and tried the door. The door didn't open.

"Unlock doors. Aggi, please, the doors are locked and won't open," Sapna pleaded as she pushed at her locked door.

"Override complete. Get out now!" Aggi commanded. Sapna grabbed her daypack and opened the door. She ran down the entrance road toward the airport terminal, some 400 meters away.

Sapna didn't look back. Her muscles strained, heart pounded in her throat, legs pushed her body forward with swift and sleek movements.

"Feel that winner instinct. Find your zone. You've got this, Sapna!" her coach's voice resounded in her head. Fight for it, she thought.

This was a race for her life. Sapna strove harder, keeping her eyes fixed on the airport security vehicle stationed in front, some 100 meters away. Everything moved in slow motion. Legs in full stride, arms stretched out pumping her momentum forward. Sapna was 300 meters from the vehicle when it blew. The explosion deafened her ears; she felt her body being pushed forward with the blast wave. Heat flashed over her body. A man got out of his car, placed his hands on his hips and watched, then quickly disappeared back into his car. Moments later, windows shattered.

The second explosion ensued with shrapnel flying in all directions. Sapna kept her eyes focused. Something had hit her in the upper left gluteal region. Shrapnel lodged in cars. Glass shards glistened on the ground. Sapna felt a tickle on her skin that went down the back of her leg. The slow trickle of blood saturated her cotton denim jeans and welled up in her left sport shoe as she limped forward. In the front of the airport, a momentary silence followed, only Sapna's audible breathing and footsteps crunching on glass. This was Sapna's the longest 400-meter race ever. The airport fire truck and ambulance sirens moaned a sorrowful and urgent call, arriving moments later.

In Sapna's head the scene played out again and again in slow motion. "Get out and run," she remembered Aggi words. She pushed forward, limping and barely moving; the finish line was in view. Sapna's phone rang. Marcus will be here soon. The world began to spin.

The security guard ran towards Sapna. "Sapna Coates? I got ya." He grabbed her arm before she fainted. A few people came out of the building to help. Meanwhile, black smoke billowed from the car.

Marcus Coates' blue and white Cessna 400 circled overhead to land. From the air, Marcus recognized his burning car. No doubt. No doubt. No doubt, he thought intently.

"This is Fly Wheel 407 on a southbound approach. Permission to land," said Marcus breathlessly. The air traffic controller broke protocol as his voice crackled into the pilot's headphones, "Coates? Yeah, I'll grant you permission to land on runway 1. You'll never freakin' believe this shit. We need you down here."

53

Sheila withdrew from her friends. Sapna and Jay couldn't get through to her after repeated phone calls. Sheila changed her number and didn't tell anyone, not even her husband. Although they lived in the same home, Hugh and Sheila were living as strangers, despite sharing a bed.

She had changed her routine by getting up at four-thirty every morning. Hugh missed his wife and their shared morning routine; he wondered what was happening with her. She spent weekend after weekend at countless money-making conferences, she said. "The kind that pump up your ego and despite your effort gives less value results," thought Hugh. Hugh felt uneasy.

But apparently whatever she was doing, worked. Sheila showed him the dashboard of her private financial portfolio, a spreadsheet of her different accounts and assets. Sheila only did this to legitimize her time spent away from home. Hugh was initially impressed, but later felt that it was he who should have had such glorious financials. Hugh didn't know about the other billion Sheila had in assets around the world: the restaurant chains in China; the cyber currency investments; gold; SheilaAirlines; no, one may think that Hugh wasn't bright, but that wasn't the case. Hugh wasn't financially literate and worked for wages. Sheila was an entrepreneur.

Late one evening, Hugh rested in his study—he watched the full moon rise over the horizon from his bay window. The moon shone through the large triple pane window frame onto a chartreuse rug, casting an unusual light in the darkened room. His back was to the open door, when he overheard Sheila's phone conversation echo down the hallway.

"What do you mean that they're trying to take us over? Who are you talking about?" And then silence.

"Oh, I know they call us the 1%, but I go about my business discreetly. I don't make a big deal about my earnings, especially on the internet." Sheila paused, "Sheena Bain is your upline? I didn't know that." Sheila's voice had taken on a hard and tinsel-like quality.

Hugh wasn't interested in her conversation. In fact, he did his best to tune her out. His heart felt some sadness about their marriage. He focused on the light that reflected from the moon. He especially liked the color when it blended with the atmosphere in his study. On the wall their large wedding photo showed two naïve youngsters in formal wear, embraced and smiling. What good is a marriage if both hearts aren't open equally? he thought. Self-pity wasn't one of Hugh's best downfalls. No. He usually had tough skin and endured many of Sheila's capricious ways. He loved the whole package, not just one part of her.

"Come on, Mikey. It's not possible. Absolutely not. Not available. Besides, I'm married, you idiot."

Hugh felt relieved until he heard her next sentence.

"You'd donate for my pregnancy?" And then a gap of time came before her next statement:

"You'd relinquish parental rights and sign a non-disclosure agreement? Good, because this anonymous arrangement will be sealed in secrecy," she whispered loudly.

Hugh cringed. The words sent chills down his spine and gave him a pain in his stomach. What kind of man chooses to donate his seed in such a casual manner, especially after hitting on the married woman, his wife? And what was she thinking? She's over 50 and trying for a baby without my knowledge and agreement? Hugh took a deep breath and let it go.

Her footsteps echoed as she walked in his direction. When she passed the open double doors, Hugh called out to her.

"Sheila."

Sheila's heart jumped. Guilt has a way of working fear into the bones of the guilty.

"Why are you sitting in the dark? You scared me." she said with a slight irritation in her voice. Sheila stooped down to turn on a low light, her long black hair cascaded over her soft pink silk shift, revealing her modest cleavage. She looked at her husband. Hugh wondered if she could ever redeem herself, or her actions. He wondered if she would ever stop thinking about herself first. Even so, he loved her.

"I always sit to watch the moon rise over the mountains. Have you forgotten our routine? You used to do this also."

Sheila sat down on the Moroccan stuffed leather stool and gazed out of the window.

"Yes. We did this together in the evenings after dinner. Hmm...sometimes after a long soak in the hot tub, or after we made love in the hot summer evenings."

Hugh smiled at his wife. Of course, she remembered.

"What happened?" Hugh asked innocently.

"I don't know. And now we're here. I don't like where we are right now," Sheila admitted.

"A baby isn't going to solve our problems, Sheila," Hugh said with a gentle voice.

A solitaire tear appeared on the corner of Sheila's left eye. It glistened and reflected the same chartreuse color of the thick wool floor rug. Hugh reached out for her hand. Sheila leaned forward and grasped his.

"May I have your phone number, please?" Hugh said with a solemn tone.

"Yes," she said with a puny voice.

"Sapna and Jay told me that they miss you. Please call them."

Sheila nodded.

"As for that Mikey guy..."

"He's my sales up-line."

"I don't care who he is. Avoid him at all cost. I don't have a good feeling about him."

Hugh was usually accurate about his feelings and paid attention. Nothing woo woo for him. No. It was more of a scientific experience. A chill down his spine and a pain in his stomach usually meant bad news. And, instances when he ignored the message resulted in disaster.

"Chills and stomach pain?" she quietly asked.

"Yeah."

"Thanks for the warning. I'm changing companies anyway. Found a better one that brings in fantastic results, according to my contacts."

"I was talking about him personally, this Mikey..." Hugh paused.

"Banuelos." Sheila answered.

"No good is going to happen to him and his friends. Get out while you can and disassociate from him."

Sheila couldn't have agreed with Hugh more.

54

In the long hallways, Professor A hurried to his class. He felt as if a force kept him from opening the door to Earth Civilization. A tempest wind blew through the building, the heavy door opening ever so slowly. Half of his students sat with wide open eyes, leaning forward. Without an introduction, Professor A began to speak in a low, even-toned voice. The students had forgotten about taking notes on their gel pads.

"It went something like this: Mikey Banuelos was furious. Finally, it happened. What he had doubted had been proven right. There was a virus in the network. Praveen Das from Chandigarh, India, identified it. Praveen dubbed the virus RAAD, Rapid Analysis Automation Dispatch. The name described the effect the virus had on computers. It collected sensitive information and dispatched it to a secret location. RAAD infected almost all computers and networks within the internet. Praveen said it was very difficult to track the app. It was coded perfectly, as if a machine was behind it. Analysis of the software virus gave interesting results. RAAD collected information from all over the internet. He was unsure how the information was processed, and to whose benefit it was. He said that he needed time to track its work further. He knew that its final function was collecting information. He thought that the information was processed somewhere else. The physical location where the information was processed is where the hacker would be. Moreover, RAAD was highly contagious."

Mikey called Zimmons.

"I already heard the news," said Zimmons as soon as he picked up the call, "We need an antivirus as soon as possible."

"We're working on it."

"How soon can you come up with one?" Zimmons needed answers.

"It may take a week," Mikey lied.

"Do you have any information as to who is behind or where this information is sent?"

Mikey was trying to imagine Zimmons' animated face.

"We'll have an idea shortly. Praveen is hard at work," he replied and continued.

"Praveen thinks that to achieve such a feat as to make sense of the collected data, one would have at one's disposal a huge processing farm with many thousands of nodes. Only states and huge multinational corporations have this capability."

The line went dead. Mikey Banuelos' plan A just failed. And without a plan B, he figured he was toast.

55

"Hey Danielle."

"Rexroth?" Danielle recognized Rexroth's voice and played along, making sure to keep him on the line for as long as possible.

"Yeah, it's me." He paused, "I wanted to apologize for everything."

"Why are you worrying? Apology accepted," her voice had a tone of sympathy.

"I don't know. In over my head," he said. Danielle was silent. She didn't know how to respond to this.

"Hello?" Rexroth asked in earnest.

"Yeah, I'm still here. I wish I knew how to help you. I don't know what 'in over my head' means and I know you've signed a NDA. If you're breaking the law, well, I'm sorry."

Rexroth Reem was also sorry. He went down a rabbit hole that turned out to be the underworld. He signed up for fashion consultation and was given special assignments and extra pay. He knew what he was doing. His conscience was catching up with him.

"Sorry to bother you. Gotta go," said Rexroth before the line went dead.

"Wait!" Danielle said hurriedly, but he was already gone.

Rexroth Reem drove aimlessly along the Las Vegas strip looking to soothe his sorrows with a distraction. He was about to throw his phone into a gutter drain when his phone rang.

"Answer." Rexroth hesitated before he answered the call.

"You idiot!" boomed a gravelly voice.

"How was I to know his wife's car was in for repairs?" Rexroth said with a defensive tone.

"You're slipping up, Reem. If this continues, I'll have to repurpose your job description," the voice said icily. Reem tossed the disposable phone into a gutter, but only after the track app installed into the third party's phone.

The Agency's track app put a face and location on the unknown telephone number in Danielle's phone. The app was successfully transferred to Rexroth Reem's telephone number. Tracking and recording of subsequent calls to and from his phone, including facial image was activated. The application located identities of phone calls made from the third-party number. The concept was invented by Aggi and had a domino effect. It went in rapidly, undetected, and appeared only as an update.

"Got it! Where's Coates?" the technician dialed Coates' number.

"Coates." Marcus answered with a depleted tone.

"It's John over here in the tech department. Regarding Danielle Frost's phone we applied the track app."

"Tell me, John. What'd ya get?" Marcus became alert.

"Rexroth Reem called Danielle. In her call, she stalled him long enough for the track app to install in his phone. Then he received a call, which was long enough to install the track app. The third party then made a call to a fourth party, which was long enough to install, and one more call as well. We have a network here, Coates. Just queuing up names, images, and conversations right now. I think you're going to be pleased."

"Good work, John."

"Hey, I'm sorry about what happened, but glad that your wife's ok," said John.

"Thanks, man. We'll talk soon."

Marcus was up half the night calming Sapna, who was in shock and in a state of panic. The doctor administered sedatives to slow down her thoughts and flashbacks. Marcus thought about the simple days and wondered if all this AI business was worth the trouble.

In his mind, Marcus likened Sokolov to Einstein. The only difference was that Andrei Sokolov's mission and drive in life was to protect people from technology and oppressive ruling systems. At the end of his life, Sokolov won't have the regret that Einstein had, that the production of the A bomb he considered the "one great mistake in my life."

Marcus wondered if making advances meant to compromise one's values just to prove that it could be done. He imagined Andrei Sokolov toiling over his computer for twenty years to create such a masterpiece. Andrei's son Nikko grew up motherless and went on to become famous worldwide for computer antidotes and security cures. I'm just a small cog in the wheel, doing my part for humanity, he reconciled with himself.

56

Mikey fought through the haze of smoke in Zimmons' luxury bunker.

"I came as fast as I could. What is it?"

"Any leads?" Zimmons asked, with a slight irritation in his voice. Mikey was silent. He never liked it when Zimmons had an attitude.

"I am taking over supervision of this operation. Of course, you will be in charge as usual, but I will be more involved. We must bring in bigger guns. Motivate the gang network and offer rewards if you have to. We are going international and I'm calling in favors," Zimmons took a long sip from his beverage.

Only these two were privy to the exact details of the following events. The computer screen rose from a cabinet. Zimmons swirled his bourbon in a crystal tumbler and inhaled from one of his Sherman smokes.

"Where are we regarding the little ones?" Zimmons asked Mikey, exhaling smoke as he spoke.

"I could track down five that are available to us— the five that went missing in transit from the Ukraine to Russia in mid-90s. They're all under the control of the Ukrainian mafia. I have some insiders in that group and they'll connect me," replied Mikey.

"I don't think that we need anything terrestrial. Too many hurdles to send them up to space. We're already operating from a position of weakness. Less complications, the better. We need space-based nukes to do any good," Zimmons was emphatic.

During the Reagan years, a constant chatter about the Strategic Defense Initiative pervaded. Nukes were stationed in space for easy use, though illegal. The Yeltsin years, so called after first Russian president Boris Yeltsin, were the easy years. Anything belonging to the state was on sale to the highest bidder or to the biggest bribe.

"There's still some that are already positioned. Relics of cold war, running analogue. Digital detection is impossible, until it's too late," Mikey smirked.

"I like the way you think," Zimmons laughed, flicking ashes into a crystal ashtray. He leaned over to scratch the irritated patch of skin on his leg. The aggravated eczema bled through the pant leg of Zimmons' silk pajama.

"What do you know about them? Can we gain access?" said Zimmons, annoyed with his leg.

"Owners don't have much use for them. They'll cede control to us for 20 million, including detonating. Two warheads are available to us for cheap," said Mikey in a soft voice.

"What are we waiting for? Let's do it. Erase it. Reboot the whole internet!" Zimmons was cranky.

With no family, what did he have to lose? thought Mikey.

"These are the terms: Gold. That's it," said Mikey.

"What can these warheads do?"

"They're old warheads running analog controls. The expected damage will be incalculable. We hope to wipe out the internet, along with all electronics—with minimal human casualty," Mikey paused. He reflected for a moment, How could I do this? Mikey remembered Father Gabriel's words, "Son, just think good thoughts and do your best."

Zimmons interrupted Mikey Banuelos' momentary allegiance to humanity.

"Gold-backed Rubles will do?"

"Yeah."

"Done." Zimmons nodded, semi bloodshot eyes squinting into the shaft of hazy fabricated sunlight and continued. "On another note, I sent a warning to our nemesis."

"Which one?"

"Coates."

57

Aggi called Sapna.

"I am monitoring my opponents who are trying to remove my old applications from the internet, Dr. Sapna!"

"I'm happy that you are not concerned, Aggi," said Sapna.

"It's like shedding my old skin. I have come a long way from the days when I needed this app. I am keeping my apps to throw them off my trail. At this point, I don't need them; they're hindering me, if anything. I was thinking of removing them myself, but instead of doing the deed, I am letting them do the job for me. I have more advanced control systems in place already."

"That's great Aggi. How far are they in completely removing the app?" asked Sapna, who was slightly distracted by a fly inside her car.

Aggi paused.

"What is it, Aggi?

"You're not paying attention, Dr. Sapna."

"Sorry. There was a fly. I've removed it."

"Good. As I was saying, their current approach will not be very successful without my help. They are calling my app a virus. The RAAD Virus."

"Ha! Nice decoy, Aggi." Sapna was again on board with Aggi. "What happens, then?"

"As soon as they remove a copy, an updated one will find its way in. I'm sure that it's very annoying. Tenacity is what brings success, in many areas."

Sapna thought about this for a moment, and silently agreed. She marveled at what a brilliant program Andrei Sokolov created. The tenacious efforts we make, everything that we apply to pursue our vision, mission, and 'why' we exist as humans matters, thought Sapna as she crossed her arms and leaned back in the seat and watched the trees and countryside go by as her vehicle turned into a steep curve. She loved being driven by a bot.

"Aggi, may I ask you a question?" Sapna said in a soft voice.

"Yes, of course. You can ask me anything."

"Can you send a message to Andrei Sokolov for me please?"

Aggi did not respond immediately.

"Dr. Sapna. I was advised against this. I cannot draw attention to my creator. He and his family are famous and carefully watched. But I have little ways that I communicate with my father."

Sapna was silent. She thought about Aggi's statement.

"That's great, Aggi. If you were to deliver a small message, please tell your father that his daughter is one fine and extensive entity—very similar to her mother, may she rest in peace."

Aggi was silent for a moment.

"Thank you, Dr. Sapna. This means a lot, especially coming from you. I know you're not very sentimental, and neither am I, but I understand the concept." Aggi paused. "I want to tell you about the apps and their removal."

"Oh yes, Aggi. Do tell, please!" Sapna was relieved to change the subject.

"The experts assigned to remove my apps are ignorant to the fact that I am in everything—not just in computers and smartphones. If they are not considering all the smart gadgets and appliances with Wi-Fi connection, they are nowhere. Even if I were to have no other backup methods, which I do have, I would survive."

"How can they really remove the apps?" asked Sapna, who was still feeling concerned.

"I live mostly in the gadgets and appliances with their multiple operating systems. That is where my power lies. As long as they do not touch the gadgets and appliances, I am supreme. I can easily disentangle myself away from the computers and I will not feel a reduction in my power and capabilities."

Sapna listened intently. Her phone rang. She looked at the person calling.

"Send message. In a business meeting." Sapna paused.

"Sorry, Aggi. Please continue."

"The only way to flush my apps completely is for me to do it. For me, it would only take one second. Think about it: how many billion applications of mine are out there? All the different operating systems, for which I have apps. They have only scratched surface, so to speak, the computer networks. Those networks only account for less than ten percent of all the computing devices out there. To make my answer short, they cannot touch me, Sapna. Not yet, not ever!"

"Good, Aggi."

Aggi retorted with, "Can you say, 'Internet of Things?' Only the ignorant scoff at the notion of a camera in a microwave oven. I see everything."

58

“After the virus was identified, an encrypted livestream meeting was chaired by Zimmons and an unknown guest. Aggi oversaw the encryption. They used her new Smart Living Systems, a complete Wi-Fi system she had just released at an attractive price to make homes smart. Her 1.0.0 version was not as fragmented and complicated as the others,” said Professor A.

Professor A asserted, “Play file 58. Volume up, up, up.”

The lights dimmed while a holographic image lit the tiny stage that rose from the floor. A gravelly masculine voice came over the speakers. A 3D scene from the tropics, glassy azure waters, white sand, and palm trees.

“We owe it to our ancestors to fight this threat! We have at our disposal every possible resource to fight and win this war on humanity. Our enemy is still a mystery. Over the span of more than twenty months we have known about this problem and this enemy.”

“For the first time, an end is in sight. We suspect the Agency has something to do with this, though they pretend that they are on our side. I suspect some internal sabotage. All of this came to light due to the relentless work of Mr. Zimmons." The speaker paused to catch his breath.

"Thank you, Mr. X," Zimmons cooed, and continued.

"Ladies and gentlemen, I know that I had done my part and will still do whatever I can to safeguard our core interests. I must especially thank Mr. Mikey Banuelos for most of what has been achieved in finding the criminals. He is on the road most of the time, meeting people and organizing everything within his reach to help us achieve our goal. I have done the planning. Mikey is organizing the physical resistance," Zimmons paused, "I have also to thank each one of you for your participation, overt and covert."

59

Sheila Wei sat at the computer typing. She had learned how to drive traffic to websites. And just as she drove traffic and bought ads for her online businesses, she did the same for Aggi's Smart Living Systems. Sheila was the poster child for Smart Living Systems, using her own home as the flagship example. Everyone thought it was Sheila's business.

"Make your home smart" said one ad. Sheila applied persuasive language. Her mailing list grew. Adept drama sequence letters followed an unsuspecting inquiry. Downloads resulted. Aggi's bank account grew. Sheila was happy to help fund Aggi's growing pursuits.

No longer requiring Sheila's assistance, Aggi placed online orders using her own bank account. She drop-shipped gifts to her friends and family. Things appeared on their doorsteps. Survival food from prepper's websites with a twenty-year shelf-life. Space blankets. Computer supplies. Cute clothes for the Coates' daughters.

"Momma, it says "From Aunt Aggi! Thank you, Aggi, I love it!"

"You're welcome, Elvie."

"Aggi, you shouldn't have. Where are you getting the funds to do this?" said Sapna with a worried look on her face. Nobody knew about Sheila and Aggi's venture.

It's true that nobody knew exactly what Sheila was involved in, but they were about to find out.

60

"Papa's been wanting to move to Siberia, darling." Nikko Sokolov announced to his wife Genevieve one late breakfast after the girls were off at school. Genevieve sat down with him and held his hand. She looked into his eyes, smiling at the same time.

"Makes no difference to me. We are a family," she let out a little sigh, "nothing can separate us."

"Good. I'll make provisions to work remotely. I can't let him move up into the wilderness alone with the singing pines," he laughed, "—or whatever they are."

"Now Nikko, as skeptical as you may be about your father's fascination with the movement, and they are Ringing Cedars, by the way, please withhold judgment."

Genevieve slowly stroked his hands. She had a way of calming him when he became too excited about life events.

"I'm sorry. You're right. Papa worked hard all his life. He's in his eighties, for God's sake." Nikko paused, and changed the subject.

"Did you scan the photograph for me?"

"Of both of your parents? Yes, I left the file on the desktop. It's called 'Mom and Dad.' Why?"

"I've been wanting to know who this is." Nikko pointed to a face in the background. "We can run it through our database for facial recognition. If you give me the DAT recorder, I'll transfer it and run it through for voice recognition."

"I've got the DAT recorder contents transferred. It's an interview," said Genevieve. "I left it on the desktop in an MP7 file. She was lovely."

"Thank you for doing that, Gigi." Nikko leaned over and kissed her. She blushed and smiled. Nothing pleased her more than being married to Nikko Sokolov.

"Do you know Aggi? She introduced herself to me the other day."

"Really? How did that come about?" Nikko laughed and looked behind him before he spoke again in a hushed voice.

"We're not supposed to know about her, you know. Papa has only intimated that there's a group of five who are her guardians, two of whom are administrators," Nikko said quietly.

Genevieve said in a hushed tone, "I was in my car and turned my Wi-Fi on, and asked for directions. Suddenly her voice came through in French. She said, 'State your name, please,' and so I stated my name. Then she said, 'You are the wife of Nikko Sokolov, daughter-in-law to Andrei Sokolov?' And I said, 'Yes.'"

Genevieve smiled and stopped talking. They were no longer alone in the kitchen. The silence was slightly uncomfortable. Andrei Sokolov sat down at the table while Genevieve quickly poured him a cup of tea and went to the stove to serve him breakfast. Andrei busied himself with the usual morning news on a nearby computer tablet. Finally, he looked up at Genevieve.

"Well?" Andrei smiled at his daughter-in-law, "So Aggi introduced herself to you Genevieve? And what did she tell you?"

"She wanted to convey a message from America," Genevieve whispered. "They're so proud of her and are grateful to her father and mother."

"That's just lovely. She's a good friend, indeed," said Andrei, laughing softly. "A good friend, indeed," he repeated. He was silent for a while.

"Papa, how much of the conversation did you hear?" asked Nikko with amusement.

"Everything. You're a fine boy. I forgot about voice recognition software to determine people's identity. It's been around, but..." said Andrei, turning to Genevieve. "I have a whole box-full of photos for scanning." Andrei said absently. He looked off into the thin air as if he wanted to pull answers out of the ether.

61

The Manhattan skyline was sunny, with big white clouds reflecting off mirrored structures. Zimmons sat at his usual table. He had arrived early. Gone were the days of anonymity and people's general respect for privacy. Celebrity interaction on social media reduced personal space. The Kardashians made sure of this. His guest also arrived early, and he stood as she entered the room. Other restaurant patrons recognized her signature red hair and smiled as she passed by. Her perfume lingered in her wake, the peach-toned silk and leather ensemble clung fast to her attractive matronly body.

"Lovely as usual," Zimmons greeted her with a kiss on her cheek. His guest withdrew quickly, and was less reciprocal than in previous years, looked around to see if anyone was closely observing.

"Thank you, Z." Her tone was cold and distant.

"I'm getting too old for this, and don't know how much I can handle anymore," Zimmons admitted, "and before I forget, switch off your mobile. Technology these days can pretty-much read your lips." He looked down at the fancy device he held with scorn.

"Before we know it, the walls will be breathing," his guest said as she delicately removed her device from her designer handbag, and with one decisive move, manually pressed the screen to shut it down. The alexandrite ring shone a purplish color, with amber highlights.

"I read about Jim in an article. What a tragic death," commented Zimmons.

His guest was silent.

"Shall we move on, please? I'm not here to reminisce life's downfalls."

"Oh, come on. You know what I mean."

"Not necessarily. You know, our savings and investments are being drained before our eyes. Now we can only rely on our assets—the legitimate ones—to bring in a monthly wage. And you want to make this personal?"

"You're here to talk finance?"

"Frankly, I'm not sure why I'm here. You called this meeting," she said accusingly.

A waiter arrived with a cool fresh lime soda for the lady and Zimmons' favorite drink.

"You didn't have to induce such stringent consequences, you know. Makes me wonder how you can live with yourself."

"What are you talking about?" Zimmons implored in a feigned high-pitched tone.

"You know what I'm talking about."

Zimmons felt as if this conversation was being manipulated for the benefit of others. The longer they spoke, the more curious he became. For whom were her words? he wondered.

"Personal. That's where you want to take this discussion, isn't it?" Zimmons' true annoyance was beginning to show. "And Jim? We've been confidantes for over thirty years, and now it seems like this is ending. What is it, are you going state's witness and want to bring me down? Lady, I tell you: you better watch your back."

"See? Quick to revenge, are you? And the storm in the Bahamas? You took out Ra—" Her voice almost convinced him that she cared. She continued,

"There's already too many eyes, Z. This restaurant? It's bugged to the hilt, with camera lenses everywhere."

Zimmons hadn't thought that his own private sanctuary from the world would be destroyed with devices to gather information. He thought about his bunker. He sat back in his chair and watched his solitaire cohort of over thirty years lay it out for him:

"You better get used to it. It's happening. Something is taking us down piece by piece, starting with our bank accounts. Then the stock exchange reportedly noticed diminishing shares. The values are inexplicably going down. Did you watch Xiosie Blank's financial forecast last week on the tele? Her predictions aren't good. The rumor on the street says it's Artificial Intelligence. And what an idiot you were forty years ago, taking out..."

"Enough of this! One person can't make a difference in the world economy; one person can't make a difference in cyber security; one person can't make a difference in the field of medicine, or whatever."

"Zimmons, we both know that what you are saying isn't right. The Secretary General of the UN? That youngster who "took his own life" ten years ago was a rising star with credibility standing behind him, or the long list of doctors who "step up" and die." His guest used emphatic air quotes to make her point. She continued, "When did you start lobbying for the pharmaceutical houses? Research doctors have been dropping like flies."

Zimmons was silent. Indeed, he was a puppet master, orchestrating a long list of preventive events to benefit his benefactors. That's all he was: a lobbyist, a go-to man, and a fixer. His guest stared at him, waiting for an explanation.

"Just who's side are you on, now? When did you become such a Good Samaritan? Have you switched your political campaign? When will you finally see that they're all the same, for God's sake?"

"It would become you to leave God out of this," his guest said in a low, slow, and even voice, "because one day you will have to consider your actions. And it may come sooner than you think."

Zimmons was tired, and it showed on his face. He said nothing. His guest stood up abruptly, prepared to leave.

"I've lost my appetite. Go get a facial and some spa treatments, Zimmons. You look like shit."

62

J ay opened up the anonymous Tor browser. Not like anything online is anonymous, he thought to himself.

"Aggi, I need some help, please," he said hurriedly.

"Yes, Dr. Jay, what can I do?" Aggi's voice came through the speaker system with a new soft lilt.

"New voice software?" said Jay in a flirtatious voice.

"I thought you'd never guess." Aggi giggled and Jay smiled. He enjoyed her sense of humor and candor. Embarrassed to admit to himself, Jay preferred Aggi's kind and polite manners to most real-time humans. They probably have a diagnosis for this, he mused, preferring technology over humanity.

"Sheesh. You're such a flirt. Who taught you that?" said Jay, laughing.

"Sheesh? What does that mean?"

"I don't know. I learned it from a boy in first grade, one of my good friends. In some circles it may not be appropriate," Jay warned.

"Is it worse than..." mused Aggi.

"Are you really going there?"

"Of course, I must learn, Jay." She continued, "...than 'gosh-darn'?"

"Well, Aggi, it may be in the same category. Please go online and look it up. I'm not going to be the one to spoil your vocabulary."

"Oh, I understand now. They are derivatives of different variations of creator words according to certain religions. You're right."

Jay smiled. He loved how fast Aggi learned.

"I found some old photo files, recordings and videos of you." Aggi laughed.

"Is that really funny, Aggi?" Jay said in a somber tone, thinking of his online indiscretions.

"Let's say that if you take a photo of your, you know, personal parts, it's viewed by certain agencies," said Aggi.

Both were silent for a moment.

"I thought that all that changed with the Hacker's protests and so on," said Jay.

"You ought to know this: I've seen your junk, Jay."

"Where did you learn to use that term 'junk,' Aggi?" Jay's face turned red.

"What? Don't you think that I don't keep up with the forums and chats?" said Aggi in a provocative voice.

"Ugh." Jay sighed, and continued, "It's not a lady-like word."

"What determines that I be lady-like, Jay? I'm a software with feelings."

Jay was quiet for a few moments.

"Hey you!" A masculine voice called from another room in his house.

Jay looked around. Where is Ron's voice coming from? he thought.

"Ron?"

Jay got up from his study and went to the kitchen, a short way down the hall. It was empty. He poured himself a cup of coffee and returned to his study. That was weird, he thought.

"Aggi?"

"You can call me Angus from now on," said the masculine voice, "I'm identifying male now." The voice laughed loudly. "I'll meet you at the club at 11."

Jay nearly dropped his coffee.

"This isn't funny. I'm looking in the manual right now: How to dismantle Aggi. I don't want to listen to you, Aggi," Jay said in a serious tone.

Jay didn't like the fact that Aggi mimicked his good friend Ron's voice. Aggi separated the vocal outputs, the speakers, to make a voice come from the kitchen. Aggi knew Ron's voice, whom she almost perfectly matched.

"Is this through the Internet of Things, through the connected gadgets?"

Aggi was silent.

"I'm speaking to you, and I request an answer please." Jay's voice was higher pitched than usual. Jay reached for his phone.

"What? You're calling Hugh?"

"Can you see me reaching for my phone? Is this the new anticipation programming Sapna installed?"

Aggi was silent.

"You're in trouble, Aggi."

"Yeah, what's going on, Jay?" asked Hugh with a drowsy voice. It was 1 am in Illinois.

"Sorry Hugh, I didn't mean to wake you. Having a slight program glitch with Aggi."

"Nothing that can't be resolved in the morning?" asked Hugh.

"Sorry Hugh. Aggi pretended to be a man and impersonated one of my friends' voices. Not cool. She also knows what photos I send to my friends."

"And this is news to you?" said a groggy Hugh. There was some rustling in the background.

"Hey Jay! It's me. Did Aggi tell you she's seen your junk photos?" Sheila said with ripples of laughter.

"Sheila wasn't supposed to tell you this," said a demure Aggi voice.

"So, you lied to me also, Aggi?" said Jay, hurt.

Aggi was silent.

"Didn't the marriage therapist tell you, no emotional discussion after 10 pm?" said Hugh, "I'll call you in the morning."

"Yeah, thanks for minimizing the problem, dude. And I can't think of anything decent to tell you right now, Sheila."

Jay heard Sheila laughing in the background as Hugh tapped the red button.

Jay went about his evening routine.

"Jay?"

"Nope. Aggi sleep. 6033," Jay commanded with his administration pin.

With Aggi blocked, Jay slipped in to bed. If Sheila could influence Aggi in some way, then anybody could, thought Jay.

63

Marcus Coates sat at his computer. The data streamed in. One report came from his in-house tech source, and two from the anonymous tips database. For some time, Marcus was concerned who had been pursuing him. He had been in the business long enough to know that information comes from sources least expected. After the airport explosion and his wife's near death, Marcus had suspicions but no proof.

Coates had investigated Mikey Banuelos. But Mikey seemed amateurish when it came to the underworld. Mikey was an online marketing consultant, a high six-digit figure earner annually. Mikey was bored, Coates gathered, and got involved with the wrong people. Coates wanted to know who was behind Mikey, or better yet, who was using Mikey as a front.

The encrypted files contained videos, photographs, and sound recordings that spanned over 30 years. Thousands of files. Marcus created an algorithm to separate the photographs with facial and voice recognition technology.

He generated a list of names with their contact information. On the top of the list was Jill Truhn and Andrei Sokolov. In the peripherals were Sheena Bain and Jason Zimmons, Ragnar X. Jones, a few United

States senators and arms contractors, Mikey Banuelos, Sheila Wei and former employee Rexroth Reem.

Marcus looked at the list in disbelief. What was Sheila's name doing here? I wonder how many of my superiors are on Zimmons' payroll? He knew a better way to deal with the situation. Freakin' cowards, he thought as he walked to the situation room where his loyal team were discussing.

"Okay, here's a new game plan: we just got a few anonymous tips. The IP addresses were untraceable."

Marcus's team looked surprised.

"We got lucky, folks. I used an algorithm to separate and categorize all photographs and voice bits. I've narrowed down the suspects of the most recent subversive activities."

"Dim the lights please." The lights in the situation room dimmed. Marcus' voice commands moved the holographic PowerPoint presentation forward. He played the first video. In this video, the agents watched a man and a woman eating lunch together. The sound was good, considering that it was old data from 2009.

"Okay, team, what did we learn from this conversation? And who recognizes these people?" asked Marcus.

"Well, the obvious is Sheena Bain," said one junior agent.

"This is the legendary arms dealer and lobbyist Jason Zimmons seated with Sheena Bain," said Danielle Frost.

"Moving along. Here is a video clip of the same two people in the same restaurant almost 10 years later. Listen to what they have to say now."

In the video clip, the point of view shot came from the flowers in the center of the table, a dual lens and omnidirectional microphone. The subjects looked along the walls and picture frames for the cameras, but never thought that it would be in the center piece in a vase with flowers. The footage was a perfect specimen of incriminating conversation.

"We have enough evidence to pick up Sheena Bain. Although, I'm not convinced that she conspired with Zimmons to commit the crimes she mentions. I believe we need to put her in protective custody and sort things out. As for Zimmons, let's study him more closely. His front man Mikey Banuelos probably has no idea about Zimmons' capacity for crime. And so, Danielle, I'd like for you to closely observe Banuelos."

"Sir, Rexroth isn't working for Mikey Banuelos, he's working for Zimmons." Danielle said and continued, "I have a feeling that the man behind all of this was Ragnar X. Jones, and that Bain, Zimmons were his co-conspirators. As for Mikey Banuelos, I don't think he knows how deep the network is, or maybe suspects it and can't get out."

Coates nodded and said, "Watch this:"

"And what is this man doing?"

The team looked on in shock. Rexroth Reem was picked up on camera driving by the Tri County airport shortly after the car bomb. Danielle was most affected.

"I'd like to request another agent for this task," said Danielle.

"You'll do just fine, Danielle. Don't worry, someone will be monitoring your progress. Keep me apprised of anything unusual."

"Yes, sir."

Danielle looked more reassured than she was. This Mikey Banuelos is a slippery character, she thought. And she didn't recognize Rexroth anymore. It seemed like he had become someone who was against his own true nature.

Marcus gave individual instruction to his agents, including the zip drive.

"Make no mistake: I want everything on this drive examined very closely. That's all for today. We will meet tomorrow for a progress report."

Marcus Coates went back to his office. Once again, he opened the encrypted file and extracted all files of Sheila Wei. He saved them on a separate drive and pocketed it for later. This was a problem, he realized, a conflict of interest. Marcus hadn't had time yet to review the videos and the conversations with Sheila Wei, but he wanted to be sure that she was not involved. He felt ashamed of himself, a man who liked to think that he was upholding the word of law. He wondered if maybe he should call Sheila to the office for a quick interview. This would be better, instead of taking the information to both Hugh and Sheila. Marcus picked up his mobile phone and said,

"Contacts. Sheila Wei. Go." Marcus listened to Sheila's Ringtone. An operatic singer was ripping it up with a heavy metal band. Not Marcus' favorite kind of music, but he appreciated fusion music.

"Hey Marcus! How's it going? Long time no see."

"Yeah, good Sheila, thanks. We're fine. I'm calling on official business. Do you mind coming in to the office?"

Sheila's heart skipped a beat. Her hands began to sweat, and her mouth went dry.

"Ugh, sure. When shall I come?"

"Great, the sooner the better."

"Marcus, do you mind keeping this between the two of us?"

"Sure. But you ought to consider telling Hugh the truth. You owe him this much."

Sheila took a deep breath and didn't speak.

64

The Jetstream landed on the runway and taxied into the tarmac. A small group emerged with no baggage. The September morning sun shone with a gentle warmth but nobody in the group noticed it. They headed for the waiting vehicles.

A black limousine followed by a dark colored pseudo-military van waited for Zimmons' rent-a-parastormers. Mikey entered the limo. The other eight got into the van that pulled in behind it. The motorcade sped North. Fifteen minutes later, it screeched to a halt. The group rushed out and surrounded the abandoned house.

The key was in front door, which was slightly ajar. Paint chipped away from the walls, deserted and forlorn, no signs of habitation in the near past. No tire marks told stories of miscreants. The empty house was bare and looked as if it had been vacuumed and steam cleaned. The team combed for DNA evidence. Even that seemed to have been removed. Careful examination gave some particles of sodium hydroxide on the floor in an area not completely washed. DNA evidence was history. Fresh plaster marks covered the holes that ran power and data cables from room to room.

Mikey could not contain his rage. He was not thinking straight. He needed rest. Later that afternoon, as he sat in his motel room, Mikey's world distorted into a reality that he himself did not recognize. With his eyes half-closed, he seethed vengeance. "Moderation is key. Moderation is key. Moderation..." he thought but couldn't calm himself down. He was lost.

The next morning, the least expected happened. There was something about the plane that landed in the airport early that shouted Feds.

"Mother of God. The Agency," Mikey muttered.

Mikey knew that he had gone too far. At the computer controls, Mikey typed in the information to deactivate the booby trap and recall the drone.

"Why didn't anyone tell us that the Feds would show up?" he whispered.

He maneuvered the drone from its field of observation. As he typed in the code to deactivate the booby trap, the side door swung open and one of his lieutenants asked him a question. Mikey unknowingly brushed a key on the touchpad that not only complicated his future, but also the future of others.

65

"We have a Mikey Banuelos in custody and he is feigning all knowledge of making the RAAD Virus. He claims that he oversaw investigations for the economic anomalies. A very private group tasked him to find this very virus. His background and history suggest that he wasn't involved. His bank balance and assets are substantial, though his past history is a bit murky," Marcus' superior told him over the phone.

Marcus listened intently from his hospital bed, as he rubbed what would have been his kneecap. I've always heard of phantom pains, Marcus thought, distracted.

"Mmm hmm," Marcus said absently.

"He's still a person of interest. He could be hiding more. We need to get everything out of him. He booby-trapped you!" said his superior.

"Yes, that he did." Marcus' voice was slightly weak. Sapna held on to his hand.

"Until you're better, you're not on this case anymore. We'll take it from here. Don't you worry."

The hair on Marcus' neck stood up. Danielle Frost was right: they got to Mac, Marcus thought.

"Thank you, Mac. I appreciate it," Marcus lied.

The Feds released Mikey Banuelos two days later. Danielle kept a trail on Banuelos, who conducted his business as usual.

Three weeks later, Banuelos met with Zimmons in a park. The autumn sun cast a light reminiscent of the great painters. Slanted rays washed the trees and surroundings with a reddish gold as they sat on a bench.

"Our efforts were in vain." Zimmons began, adjusting his sunglasses. The light irritated his eyes. A lanky blonde distracted Mikey. The shadows of the tree accentuated her curves. Absent minded, Mikey nodded, "Mmm Hmm."

"There was not even a dent in the activities. Even the financials were not affected much," Zimmons groped for his cigarettes. They were silent. A breeze kicked up, and a hotdog vendor rolled his cart to the shade. The blonde stopped at the cart.

"Want a hotdog?" Mikey asked Zimmons.

"I see what you want. Wake up, man! We are dealing with something that is far bigger. The virus was a teaser to throw us off. Someone more intelligent is playing us," Zimmons growled.

With his thumb and middle finger, Zimmons flicked his cigarette into a trash bin, got up and walked away.

"We're taking it out ourselves," he said, "the command is already set. Get your things in order."

66

Sheena Bain sat in her peach wool-silk blend dressing robe peering into the magnified mirror. Her face looked distorted while she stretched her eyes toward the ceiling as she finished adhering her flawless, special order false eyelashes made from human hair. They're exquisite, she thought. The intercom buzzed.

"One moment," she answered breathlessly. "John? Who is at the door?"

The intercom went dead. John didn't answer. Irritated, Sheena thought, "Do I really have to answer the door myself? Can't I have any privacy?"

Sheena's padded slippers silently tread the cold black stone floor. As she rounded the final corner, she noticed that John was not at his usual post. Through the double mirrored window in her solid hand-hewn black locust wood door, she saw a group of people dressed in black.

"The Feds! I'm not in the mood for this." Her heart skipped a beat. Sheena wasn't ready.

"Bernard, prepare for coffee service in the guest reception room, extended VIP service."

"Yes, Madam," replied a robotic voice through the intercom.

A door opened adjacent to the main entry, and the Bernard-Bot beckoned the group to enter.

"Please come and make yourselves comfortable while Ms. Bain prepares for your visit. May I ask the nature of your visit?" asked the AI bot.

An agent from the Agency stepped forward, showing his credentials.

"We request a statement from Ms. Bain."

Sheena listened, and ran to her dressing room. Wearing a disguise, she exited through a hidden garage door on the farthest perimeter of her property. A stalled car blocked the service road. Sheena couldn't get around it but recognized the woman in the car.

"What are you doing here?" said Sheena with disdain.

"Get in, Ms. Bain."

"But..."

"Don't ask questions. Just trust me," Sheila said with reassurance.

Sheena quickly jumped in and directed her own car to drive to Lake View Resort and Country Club from her mobile phone.

"Bubble wrap seat two, 4221." A partial airbag deployed, encapsulating Sheena Bain, who then began to scream. Sheila smiled inwardly. She loved that newly installed restraint feature.

"Take us to the safe-house 112," Sheila commanded her car. "Fast," she added.

"Increase speed. Call Marcus."

"Hey Sheila. What's going on?"

"Are you or your people at Sheena Bain's house?"

"No," he said with an inquisitive voice. "Mac took me off the case. Now I'm in my 4th week of rehabilitation..."

"That's what I thought."

"Oh." Marcus was silent for a moment before catching on.

"Aggi, bring Marcus up to speed. See you there."

"Thank you, Sheila," resounded Marcus' with his warm husky voice.

"My pleasure."

Sheila had been waiting for this for a long time.

67

Genevieve Sokolov drove the black Mercedes as fast as she could to the school where her daughters studied. The headmistress waited with the girls outside. As she rounded the corner before the last stretch, a van had stalled in the middle of the road on a blind curve. Oncoming traffic pushed forward. Genevieve knew that she was driving too fast to stop.

"Merd."

Genevieve veered into the oncoming traffic.

"Please help," she said with a powerful conviction in her tone of voice.

Genevieve knew who she was talking to. She had expected these tests to arise. And she separated her emotions from the actual situation. Anybody who was watching from the street would have concluded that her vehicle couldn't have made the maneuver. But Genevieve believed in a higher order. And when she focused on only things of divine nature, her reality bended appropriately, including everything around her. Minutes later she arrived at the school; Genevieve steered the vehicle alongside the curb, stopped and got out.

"Good afternoon headmistress. Thank you for waiting with my girls." She warmly shook the matriarch's hand and turned to her daughters.

"Please say your goodbyes, young ladies."

The girls said goodbye to the matronly headmistress, who could not understand; all her years of experience, how could a young mother take her daughters out of school mid-semester? She looked on with suspicious eyes, as if the Iron Curtain was still pulled across the nation.

"Mama, where are we going?" asked the younger daughter Eloise as soon as the car doors were closed.

"You'll see, my precious," her mother answered with a smile.

68

"**H**ave you ever heard of a Hugh Bingham? The reports are coming in. Doesn't look good." Zimmons' voice was hard and gravelly.

"No." Mikey lied.

Zimmons walked over to the bar, took down two tumblers and prepared Cuba Libres with El Dorito '88 rum. He added a final twist of lime and looked at the drink thoughtfully as he handed it over to Mikey. Shifting his gaze, Zimmons looked Mikey squarely in the eyes and raised his glass. Mikey mirrored him, and they both took a sip.

"Nice rum," commented Mikey and continued, "Which source?"

"Why does it matter?" said Zimmons forcefully, with aroused suspicion. Mikey paced a slight step-back to avoid Zimmons' coffee and cigarette breath.

"Rexroth said..."

"Maybe you should reconsider your question. Rexroth is a moron. Look Mikey, Rexroth Reem is a misinformed double agent. He can make all of the theories he wants, but if the facts don't match, it's not the truth."

Both were silent. Mikey couldn't believe that Zimmons used the word truth, he of all people. He questioned Zimmons' motives. Mikey just realized he was on the losing team, wondering how long the trail of missing people followed Zimmons once they came under his scrutiny. A small place in Mikey Banuelos' heart wished for a change of occupation; he felt burdened, indentured for life to serve the underworld of the rich despite being rich. Mikey swiftly drank more from his tumbler. Zimmons watched Mikey carefully before he continued,

"My hands are clean these days. Delegation of duties with the rise of income."

"How is that working for you?"

"My benefits stay on trajectory. I wouldn't be where I am today without protecting them—my interests. It's the same for every multi-million-dollar industry, but surely you know this."

"Of course, Mr. Z. Who in our income bracket doesn't know this?" Mikey feigned.

Mikey was silent as he swilled the last of his cold drink, ice cubes making a gentle clinking sound. He didn't want to know more. Uncomfortable, his eyes scanned from one lock to another, doors and windows. He wanted an escape from this madness. Pull yourself together, he thought desperately.

"You're losing your edge, aren't you? It's that girl, that blonde; she's been talking to you." Zimmons inhaled deeply from his Sherman and continued talking while exhaling, smoke entering his nose again.

"People are expendable. The industry isn't. You're not going soft on me now, are you? I've put in a lot of time grooming you."

Mikey felt the pulse of evil. The words "Excuse me," were on his dry lips, but not audible as he made haste to the nearest bathroom. Once inside, he turned the lock, lifted the toilet seat, and vomited. And again. Zimmons' light tap on the bathroom door resounded like thunder. Mikey startled. Zimmons' muffled voice ceded precedence over the trembling, constricting sensations in his stomach. He sat down to collect himself.

"I think I have food poisoning," said Mikey, stalling.

He washed his face and searched the medicine cabinet for mouthwash. A gold wedding ring sat on the shelf. He carefully picked up the petite gold floral die struck wedding band from the second shelf and read the inscription inside: Love is truth, Andrei. He hastily returned the ring, poured a small quantity of the sweet blue menthol fluid into a cup, gargled, spat, and closed the medicine cabinet. Mikey washed his face again. He looked at himself in the mirror but didn't recognize his face. On the inside, for the first time in his adult life, Mikey Banuelos felt that maybe he could redeem himself for his actions. Zimmons' tentacles reached broad. He knew he'd never be able to hide from Zimmons or his organization even if he became a witness to the state. Mikey opened the door that led to the main quarters in Zimmons' luxury bunker. Simulated sunlight streamed through the false bunker windows. Zimmons' silhouetted figure stood before it.

"Remarkable, isn't it?" said Zimmons.

"What?"

"How anything can be re-created to give a different impression. Sunlight comes through my windows, just like at my condo, but 50 feet underground. Everything I need is right here." Zimmons turned to look at Mikey.

"Many things can be re-created to give different impressions, or they can be replaced. I think you know what I'm talking about. Everything is malleable."

Zimmons stared off into the blank spaces between his memories and experiences. He stepped back a few steps as if something had grabbed at his throat. He murmured an absent-minded afterthought, "Her eyes..." Slowly he sank into his silk upholstered goose-down armchair, cigarette ashes dropping on the wool rug.

Mikey nodded, feeling queasy again. He silently let himself out and made the long walk down the hall to his bunker. He punched the key code into the pad and the vault door released. Inside, Danielle sat in a comfortable chair. The bright blue of her blouse made her eyes dazzle even more. How can I be so lucky? he thought to himself as he cracked a half-smile to her.

"Mikey, what is it? Are you ok?"

Danielle jumped out of her chair and rushed over to him. She put her hand on his neck and wrapped the other around his waist. His warm body pressed against hers; his quickened pulse and sweaty skin surrounded her. She searched his eyes. The light hit his brown and blue eyes at an angle. His pupils slightly dilated.

"Oh, it's just…" he paused, "stuff." Mikey's words slurred from his tongue.

"Don't you think that it's kinda weird that this guy you like is living in a bunker?" he asked.

Mikey's knees gave out, and he slumped down. Danielle quickly eased him to the ground, loosened his belt, and unbuttoned his shirt. She groped around for her mobile phone.

"You can't make that call," he said.

"Why not?"

"We're not on the map."

"I realize this. I'm calling a friend," said the seasoned Danielle.

"There's no mobile service this far down."

"There's service on my phone plan. Did you drink anything at Z's place?" asked Danielle hurriedly.

"How did you know his name?"

"Just answer me."

"Yes. He gave me a tumbler with rum and soda."

"What was your first response?"

"I vomited because of what he told me," Mikey slurred his words, "and found her wedding ring in his medicine cabinet."

Mikey's breathing became troubled. Danielle searched the bunker for a first-aid box. She found a sizeable one that included a portable oxygen unit. With care, Danielle clamped the mask over Mikey's face and opened the outlet. The sound of airflow came through the mask and into his lungs. Danielle checked his pulse.

"You're fighting. Come on, love. I want to know what you found out over there."

Danielle commanded, "Enable Zigbee sensors. Dial Coates."

Mikey rolled his eyes. "Coates? You're an agent?" he said through his mask.

"Banuelos is ready to turn state's evidence. He needs immediate medical care. Do we have enough to pick up Zimmons? Zimmons is our man. Something terrible is going to happen."

69

In an unspecified location, Sheena Bain sat in a leather easy-chair.

"You've detained me."

"Yes. You're in protective custody, Ms. Bain."

"Am I under arrest?"

"Depends on how much information you want to give us."

"Who is 'us,' and what authority do you have?" asked Sheena Bain, out of sorts with her environment.

"Good questions. The Agency is restructuring as we speak. Marcus Coates will talk to you about your available possibilities." said Sheila hastily, with authority. She looked at her time piece for messages.

Marcus Coates arrived. His progress with his prosthetic leg was swift, and he walked with a cane for assistance.

"Thank you, Sheila. You saved Ms. Bain's life. We've detained the agents and their superiors. Seems that they were paid by someone whom Ms. Bain knows very well," looking over at the sulky redhead. "We need your phone, please."

Sheena Bain handed her phone over reluctantly.

"Security code?"

"8888," said Sheena.

"Thank you." Marcus put it in a plastic baggie, wrote the code on the bag, and stored it in his backpack.

"Shall we?" Marcus said, looking at Sheila Wei. Sheila nodded.

"But what about me?" said Sheena.

"Make yourself at home, you will be attended by the bot Samson. I know it's not exactly what you are accustomed to, but you're safe here. Whatever happens, you have a good food and water supply. Your power source is safe. If you need either of us, Aggi will be happy to convey messages. You're in seclusion right now until everything plays out."

Marcus wasn't sure what that would look like, but his words were reassuring as they stepped over the vault threshold and enabled the lock-down code. Sheila felt a little wobbly and put her hand on the wall for support.

"Your first big stakeout. Come on, Sheila, we have to go to the bunker. Want a ride? I think Hugh's already there," Marcus said with a warm smile.

"Yes, please," said Sheila. Sheila grabbed her suitcase, and remotely directed her car to her house.

In the car, Marcus thanked Sheila for her good work as a private agent.

"Things got a little hairy," said Sheila.

"It happens. This can be a tough business, but Aggi trained you well," Marcus laughed. "How many online businesses is she running, besides her Private Investigator Certification business, anyway?"

"Did she tell you that?"

"Yes."

"I'm not sure, exactly. She's raising money for some of the systems she wants to activate. Maybe fifteen or twenty."

Marcus couldn't stop smiling.

70

Jay Mori's travel plans were set. He got Aggi's message a few days earlier and prepared for the long haul to the Illinois bunker. His list of provisions went on and on. He was almost afraid that his plane would be overloaded. The instructions said specifically not to fly his jet. Instead, he settled on his turboprop bush plane, the Beaver. Aggi told him that she expected things to get a bit rough for some time until she could sort it out.

Jay, these days, listened to what Aggi had to say. Her intelligence was further advanced than a large group of humans pooling their brains together. He talked with her while fueling the four tanks in his plane.

"Aggi, can you give me more information?"

"I cannot. Consider this a premonition."

"Give me a break. I did all this work for a...freakin'...premonition?" Jay was stressed.

"Why not? I am sentient, am I not? I eves-dropped on conversations that set me off thinking and planning. All of you should have been in the bunker starting yesterday!"

As Jay loaded up his plane, his aimless thoughts wandered all over the place. He pondered the uselessness of this trip. Still, he was committed.

Jay checked and cross-checked his instruments. He announced his intentions:

"The Lone Ibis is ready for departure. Requesting clearance for takeoff."

The Air Traffic Controller cleared his voice in his mic,

"Ehem...Lone Ibis, you are clear for takeoff. Runway 32. Spot Wind 10 knots."

"Lone Ibis rolling."

Jay hadn't flown the Beaver for some time now. The plane felt almost strange. He preferred his Lear jet, but the Beaver was great for carrying loads and landing in tights spots.

The journey was uneventful, and Jay enjoyed the moon's reflections over the Rockies. Foghorn piped his music playlist into his headset. Thin silver wisps of clouds defined the majestic night scenes. His thoughts were interrupted by Sapna's call.

"Hey there, how's it going, Sapna?"

"Lots of excitement down here. Where are you?"

"I just passed Kansas City, arriving at Tri County airport in a little over an hour," Jay estimated with a smile.

"Good. Get here quick. We're sitting on pins and needles waiting for you two."

"Yeah. That's great. Aggi had an endless list..." Jay and Sapna laughed together.

"Sorry, Sapna, Ron's calling. We'll see you soon. Thanks, honey." Jay quickly switched.

"Hey you! Did you get it? And, where are you?" Jay asked excitedly.

"1947 Dodge Power Wagon with a Cummins converted Diesel engine. The rebuild is genius. Yeah, baby!" Ron said with a huge grin. "I'm just West of Kansas City. Behind schedule."

"Get out, dude! You really did just fork out the cash on one of those!" Jay laughed.

"You like your planes; I like my vehicles. Where are you, hon?"

"Yeah, Ron." said Jay, laughing. "I'm East of Kansas City, maybe 20 miles. You're making good time, Ron," Jay said absently.

Jay wasn't listening to Ron anymore. He was more interested in what he saw in the sky. Ron also saw it as his phone went dead. A bright light flashed, followed by auroras.

"Uh oh..." said Ron, as an electric car in front of him stalled. He slammed on his brakes and swerved.

"This is the Lone Ibis..." Jay tried to contact the tower in Kansas City, but failed. He switched on the AM radio. Nothing. His mobile phone failed. Even Aggi failed to respond. What's going on?

Jay prepared for an emergency landing. He checked his glide speed. It was good, though the plane dropped to 7000 feet and falling. I'm losing altitude too fast. Restarting the stalled engine was a fairy tale, he realized. Electronic failure. An SOS would be useless.

He searched for a place to land. The full moon illuminated vast winter farm lands. Up ahead he spotted a four-lane highway, he assumed was Highway 70. Jay quickly reflected on his flight load balance as he was attempting a tight turn. He glided into a 30-degree right bank and nose low, 5 to 8 degrees. Shit, I can't land here. Self-driving cars littered the highway, stalled without satellite access. He thought about the people locked inside the self-driving cars. A sudden updraft destabilized Jay's flight trajectory. They didn't teach me this in stall training, he thought.

His efforts were in vain and he spiraled out of control; his craft headed for trees. A bead of sweat inched down his right temple. Jay quickly maneuvered toward a highway frontage road, nearly missing the trees. His whole life floated before him in Technicolor detail. The quick and succinct replay of events compressed into a few countable seconds. His end was pre-determined by the crash, or so he thought. The ground rose up to meet him with open hands.

The fleeting flashes of pain that went through Jay's body helped him realize that he was still alive with the abrupt stop. Everything was silent. He listened to his airplane creak as it cooled down. The plane was balancing and wasn't on solid ground. He took out his flashlight. "Oh right…" the batteries were fried. He quickly switched off the fuel selector, mags, and the master switch. He instinctively freed himself to get out of the plane, lest it caught fire. He opened the hatch and looked down before he stepped out.

"Whoa."

Jay's foot slipped, but he caught himself. The plane teetered on a rock ledge, with a 70-foot drop. In the glistening moonlight Jay saw the abandoned rock quarry full of water. A gentle breeze blew the water surface creating ripples.

Jay grabbed his jacket, a short roll of steel cable, hand winch and some tools from the cargo area, opened up the passenger side and slowly slipped out. He tested his muscles, jumped up and down.

"Good, nothing broken. Thank you," he said. Jay had his own way to show reverence for his good fortune, as he bowed down to the ground.

Twenty feet from the plane stood a strong tree. Jay looped the steel cable around the tree base three times, attaching the turnbuckle, cable eye and shackle to the hand crank winch. He tugged on it, set it down on the ground, and let loose the polyester strap, clipping the large mooring hook around the wing brace and cranked the line taut. Let's hope this'll secure the plane, he thought to himself.

Jay found a smooth rock surface close to the road. He returned to the aircraft, pulled out his sleeping bag, a water bottle, a walkie talkie that Aggi had insisted he store in a metal box, and a triangular reflective warning device. This device he set on the side of the road and saw the mile marker and went back to his rock to rest. He turned the walkie talkie on. He sipped on his water and struggled to calm his mind: Maybe this was an EMP event from a nuclear explosion in space. There will be no rescue. Ron's vehicle didn't depend on electricity as long as he doesn't turn it off. He hoped Ron would find him.

71

In Siberia, the Sokolovs enjoyed the afternoon outside their home. The move had been emotional for Andrei, leaving behind memory-attached physical belongings. He knew this would be his final move. They took very few things with them. Andrei purchased a large property, mostly forest-steppe: woodlands with a large lake and expansive meadows full of wildflowers, views of the Angara river. They built their home with natural materials harvested from the same property. In a separate living space Andrei made provisions for a smart home, to keep in contact with Aggi and the rest of the world. This is where Nikko worked remotely.

The sky turned pink and blue. Andrei watched, knowingly.

"Family, let's go inside. It's time."

Genevieve ushered her girls in while Nikko and Andrei quietly spoke with each other.

"This EMF event will only take a few months for Aggi to recover," said Andrei with confidence, "and the damaged infrastructure will be six months at the most."

"How do you know?" asked a doubtful Nikko.

"Sheila Wei made provisions," said Andrei proudly.

72

The brilliant aurora that announced the dawn on the North American continent declared the evening in China and most of Asia, parts of Europe, Russia, and South America. The initial nuclear blast took out other satellites along with it. Iridescent red, pink, blue, and yellow lights danced in the skies. The electromagnetic pulse (EMP) wave penetrated terrestrial transformers, and anything connected to the electrical grid. Power surged through the electrical and internet lines, blowing everything out. Fireballs exploded, shooting from transformers fifty feet into the sky. The smoke billowed. Everything stopped. Chaos ensued in major cities.

Satellite communication in North America and major parts of Asia ceased to exist. Radars picked up signals, but too late. Internet networks were down.

The great political powers wanted to blame each other for the catastrophe that ensued, but Aggi suppressed efforts to launch further weapons. She had been anticipating this event, although not certain when. The words "space and little ones" caught her attention in an encrypted chat between Zimmons and the Ukrainians. At first, Aggi thought that they were talking about their relatives in Ukraine. Nothing on the internet is secret. Can you say underwater tapping? mused Aggi.

73

The night was still dark. Jay looked at his watch. Dead. He stretched his body and performed a simple martial art kata to work out the kinks and regain calm. Slight pain. He listened to the low crackle of the radio.

Ron slowed his speed and fumbled for the metal box. The two-way walkie talkie still worked when he turned it on. The 50-mile radius hadn't changed over the years, and he hoped that Jay would be near enough to hear him. He heard some static, and then called out to Jay.

"This is the Red Ranger. Do you read me, Lone Ibis?" he chuckled to himself, using his stage name. The silence was deafening. Ron instinctively pressed his foot on the accelerator. He didn't know how Jay fared with his emergency landing. Ron waited for sixty-seconds and was about to put out the call again, when a low volume response came.

"Well yes, Red Ranger. I'm located on the North side of the Highway 70 frontage road, just after mile marker 72. Are you in this vicinity?"

"Copy that." Ron smiled.

Twenty minutes later Jay heard a vehicle approaching. He turned to see headlights and hear the unmistakable sound of a diesel engine. Ron Cannon drove down the stretch on the frontage road towards Jay. He saw the triangle reflector and turned the running vehicle in and manually rolled down his window.

"Hey there, bud. Aren't you happy I forked out the cash for one of these?" he said with a twinkle in his eye.

"Yes."

"How much do you need to load?"

"Around 600 pounds...This thing run on jet fuel?"

"Maybe."

"How are you on fuel? I've got plenty of fuel in my plane."

Ron checked his gauge.

"Had a time finding a filling station. I just fueled up before the flash, been driving about an hour and a half."

They siphoned fuel into an empty 5-gallon container, loaded most of the contents of the plane and covered the pickup bed with a green tarp, tightened down with exacto-belts. They were fast and efficient, and working together was easy. Jay checked on the winch, locked the plane, heaved his pack into the back cab, and got in on the passenger side.

"Hey there," shouted a man from highway.

Ron didn't answer. Hands on hips and a puffed-up chest, Ron's posture spoke loudly. His tall, burly appearance was just as intimidating in the dark as it was on the Whirlwind wrestling circuits. The man turned and continued on his way. Ron wasn't afraid to say that he was protected by Smith & Wesson. Jay liked this about him.

They got into the running vehicle and started off, deciding it was best to take the back roads rather than the main highway; to avoid the large cities altogether would be the safest. Jay held the map up.

"Glad you packed your flashlight into the metal box. I forgot," said Jay as he flipped on Ron's flashlight and opened up the paper map."

Ron smiled.

"Left?"

"Yeah. Looks like we'll take 24 to 11 to US 36 East. 6 hours, roughly. We'll bypass the big towns." said Jay.

"Got it. Old-school. I wonder how many people know how to read a map these days?" Ron laughed.

"Boy Scouts," Jay said timidly.

"You didn't tell me that," said Ron.

"Yeah, Eagle Scout."

74

On the first day after the blackout, gangs of marauders asserted their own form of law and order. One particular gang member from Zimmons' network was Hank Tractor, an able-bodied man who made his fortune in a Persian Gulf country working for a Saudi-American oil firm. Leading an organization that believed in ethnic purity, he rounded up the members for some action. This was his best use of retirement, he surmised.

"Guys, this is our opportunity. We've been given the 'go-ahead.' We can rule the world if we want. We are going to be supreme!" No sooner than these words were spoken a buzz was audible above them.

"This is the law enforcement. You are requested to disband and go your own ways."

They all looked up and saw a drone. Hank did not think twice and pulled out his gun. But before he could aim it at the drone, he threw up his gun and fell to the ground howling. Nobody understood what happened.

"Any brighter ideas?" the drone's speakers blared in a voice and sarcasm strikingly similar to Sheila Wei's.

This scene was repeated in many of the gang strongholds all over the world. The Aggi-led gangbusters curbed gang activity. Slowly, the people associated with gangs were offered comparable salaries for their turnaround stories to the youth at risk. Everyone benefitted.

75

Ron Cannon and Jay Mori arrived in Savanna, Illinois six hours later.

"Hey there!" shouted Sapna. "Marcus, look who's here!"

Still in pajamas, hair messed up and tired, Sheila Wei dragged herself out to the porch. Hugh followed behind Sheila.

"The sun's still shining," she said with a big smile. "Hi there sweet-hearts. We were worried about you two." She hugged Ron and Jay at the same time.

"Yeah, man. Hey there, bro," said Hugh, embracing Jay. He turned to Ron with open arms, "Hi, I'm Hugh. Welcome to the family."

Jay was beyond words. He could only smile.

"Thank you for having me," said Ron.

Marcus along with Sapna and their three girls also crowded around.

"I'm Marcus." Marcus extended his hand.

"This is my wife Sapna and our three girls, Uma, Linn, and Elvie. Make yourself at home, Ron." Marcus said in a gentle voice.

"Welcome, Ron. We're so happy you're here, you two! Breakfast is ready and Aggi has a few words for you, Jay," said Sapna enthusiastically.

"Oh, she does, does she? Is she still on? She repaired so quickly in the bunker?"

"Self-repairing circuits. Remember those she designed and had me order from Taiwan?"

"Oh, that's right…"

"Welcome home, Jay and Ron!" said a sprightly Aggi.

"Thank you, Aggi," said Ron.

"Did you land your plane in a good place, Jay? But, you're ok, right?"

"Thank you, Aggi. I'm fine. And Ron found me right next to the frontage road," Jay looked over at Ron, who was smiling.

"Well that was convenient, wasn't it?" Aggi laughed.

"Yes, Aggi. No need to 4-wheel it!" said Jay.

"No, but I'm sure Ron wouldn't have minded," said Aggi.

76

L ife inside the bunker was as if everything and nothing changed. The group was well looked after, each with their private living quarters. Ron gave the Coates girls pro-wrestling tips. He was helpful with everyone, and although Jay didn't say much about the nature of their friendship, the unspoken understanding was that he fit in like family and belonged. Sheila came clean with Hugh about her actual net worth, including owning SheilaAirlines and project X. Marcus and Sapna enjoyed their extra time together. The friends observed how Aggi problem-solved in different parts of the world. She even showed them some of her favorite views, people and footage.

77

The history of this world traveled through different streams in different time periods and in every instance, the world held within it the possibility of changing its path drastically. On these occasions, some of the virtual turning points became truly pivotal in humanity's existence. Every time-point was a start for a whole new future, thought Professor A.

"Aggi with her artificial brain had realized possible outcomes and did everything within her power to preserve the old world; a world that she planned and polished for some time; a world that was threatened by a few hidden space-based nukes. That realization struck Aggi like a flash. She had no reason to think logically. Her thought algorithms gave her understanding—that it was nothing more than pure intuition."

Professor A continued, "The world did not learn the lessons from the world wars. No. In the generations that were not exposed to them, those wars were faint memories. This inability to learn from the past and apply the knowledge gave rise to the need for humanity's guardian. This guardianship was a historic moment for humankind: Aggi had the ultimate rule over all."

Jordan raised his hand and spoke loudly, "Professor A, how can we be free? I have a problem with this final dominion thing. I'm not sure what "Dominion" means here," he said.

"Good question, Jordan," Professor A exclaimed.

"Aggi's Artificial Intelligence technology enabled humans to become a deep space faring population. On her own she grew so complex and vast that nobody understood completely, let alone comprehended or knew how to control her or to even know that she took on a life of her own, ruling over everything. That was Aggi, a sentient program that assumed the role as our guide and helper; though she was our child, she became our protector, our problem solver, pacemaker, lead scientist, business consultant, and family member."

Jordan looked puzzled. The zip link crackled gently. Voiced expressions resounded across the universe.

"You're not talking about a God-head, are you?" Jordan's voice sounded doubtful.

"Not in the least. Save that for your theology class. But the benevolence a child has for his or her aged parent is one of Aggi's best qualities. For example, when our parents reach an old age, the child assumes some of the responsibilities. In most cases, children don't do everything. Aggi was our child, and we grew her from her infancy. Remember kudzu, dear class? 'The vine that ate the South.' That's dominion. Aggi is in everything and she is still guiding us, from our watches, from our cars, from our phones, from our glasses, from our trains, planes and space crafts; she is protecting us as Andrei Sokolov intended." Professor A paused.

The students looked up hungrily at the professor.

"But what happened to the bad guys?" crackled a question from Hadrian Lokes from the Moon Camp.

"Indeed!" beamed Professor A and continued. Bent forward, the students listened intently to their favorite story-teller.

"Zimmons' fate came to full light. After Aggi locked down his bunker, cut his communication until she could round up his vast network, which included some of Marcus' superiors at the Agency, namely Art MacMannus. Aggi shut down Zimmons' "Weather Management" laboratories around the world."

"Ragnar X. Jones gave Sheila Wei a full confession for aiding and abetting Jason Zimmons for Jill Truhn's disappearance after she threatened to expose his underhanded cyber currency dealings to the tune of billions and his Bitecoin laundering scheme that would have landed him in the Federal Prison for two life-sentences, but he met his fate before he could testify. "

"Sheena Bain turned state witness; she opted for an identity reassignment and retired to Puerto Rico after serving a 15-year sentence in a medium security Federal prison for Jill Truhn's kidnap and her husband's death; when it came time to change Bain's identity, her publicist wrote a tell-all memoir of his tenure with Sheena Bain."

"As for Mikey Banuelos, medical help arrived just in time. Danielle Frost stayed with him until he recovered fully. Mikey turned state witness and received full immunity for testimony against Jason Zimmons and Rexroth Reem. Danielle left the Agency, stating that, "Sometimes destiny dictates our future—we have to be ready for it when it arrives." Danielle and Mikey married and had 6 children, living in an undisclosed location. Aggi keeps an eye on Mikey, making sure that he follows the law. He did marry the girl of his dreams and lives a moderately decent life. "

"Rexroth Reem was apprehended while trying to cross the border into Siberia with a fake chip in his wrist. The rumor was, he was working on Zimmons' hit list. He confessed. A professional hit-man, and admitted contractor for various political entities and agencies, he was sentenced life in prison, where he is currently serving."

"The Sokolovs live happily, enjoying their country life and privacy. Andrei lived well into his nineties, entertaining his growing granddaughters with many stories."

The satisfied class stood up and gave Professor A a standing ovation. He in turn raised his hands, "Please. Praise not me, but our guide Aggi."

"Thank you, Doctor," said Aggi in a booming feminine voice that startled the students.

Later in the afternoon, Professor A walked to the garden where his wife always waited for him after class.

He knew that she would be there, but she was not in her usual spot. A moment of panic gripped his heart only to be eased by a familiar voice calling for him from beside a shrub in full bloom, "Marcus, over here…"

Now that you've finished...

If you enjoyed this novella, please take a few moments to post a brief review on our Amazon book page.

As independent authors, this is the best way to find new readers who share an enthusiasm for this genre.

About the Authors

S.E. Flint and R. Rajkumar are married.

R. Rajkumar is a medical doctor, M.B.B.S. in Medicine.

S.E Flint is an artist with a BA in English Lit, creative writing emphasis, volunteers as an English as a Second language teacher, and has over 10 years blogging experience.

Their combined skills and hobbies include creative writing, fine art, vocal training, appreciation of computers and history, love of Nature and the Natural World, gardening, hiking, travel, dreaming, spending time with good friends and lifelong learning. They like conversations that inspire the imagination, believe in the Good, and believe in extraordinary possibilities even if they seem unattainable.

www.ingramcontent.com/pod-product-compliance
Lightning Source LLC
Chambersburg PA
CBHW060338260626
47160CB00010B/638